# MARVELLOUS MARY BROWN AND THE MYSTERIOUS MANHUNT

## BERNICE BLOOM

Bernice Bloom

# DEAR READERS

Welcome back to the world of Mary Brown Mysteries. This is the follow-up book to *Marvellous Mary Brown and the Mysterious Invitation*.

It can be read as a stand-alone story, but is better enjoyed after the Mysterious Invitation book, available here:

UK: My Book
US: My Book

In Mysterious Manhunt, we join our gorgeous heroine as she is relaxing at home with her boyfriend Ted.

It's been a year since she received an invitation to the funeral of Reginald Charters, a man she'd never heard of. She was persuaded to go to the funeral by his lawyers who insisted that Reginald had begged, on his deathbed, for her and five other people to attend.

Intrigued by this, she headed for Gower in south Wales.

There she met up with the other five people who'd been invited to the funeral. They had no idea why they had been invited either.

Over an intense couple of days before the funeral, they had to work out why they had been chosen to attend, in order to inherit his wealth. There were lots of twists and turns along the way, as Reginald teased them from beyond the grave, and in the end only five of them inherited money. Julie was chosen as the least deserving person in the group and left with nothing.

While they were at the funeral, they were told that the Gower family, who Reginald was desperate to leave money to, could not be found so their share of the money was kept in an account for when a member of the Gower family could be located.

So, now we return to Mary's flat. It's been a year since the funeral. She and Ted are relaxing at home.

I hope you enjoy the book.

BBx

# PROLOGUE

*M ysterious Invitation WhatsApp Group*

**Simon Blake**

Dear all, I sincerely hope you're keeping well. Did you know that next weekend marks a year since we met up in Gower for Reginald's funeral? Can you believe that? A year! Goodness, doesn't time fly? Kind regards, Simon B

**Mike Sween**

Hi mate, a year? Hope you're good.

**Simon Blake**

Yes, I'm very well, thank you, Mike. I wondered whether

anyone fancied meeting up to celebrate the occasion and to raise a toast to Reginald? Kind regards, Simon B

**Sally Bramley**

Hi Simon, Oh yes, I'm up for that. Are you thinking of us all going back to Gower Farm Hotel? The one we all met at before? It would be lovely to see everyone xxxx

**Mike Sween**

I will if I can, mate, but got so much work on at the moment. Let me have the details and I'll try. Nice to hear from you

**Simon Blake**

Dear all, That sounds like it might work, then. I will await messages from the others, and see whether anyone else fancies coming along, and will arrange something. I'll have a think about where would be a good place for us all to meet. It would be lovely to see you all again. Kind regards, Simon

# CHAPTER 1

# $\mathcal{M}$ary's House: Present Day

Have you ever watched one of those daft shows from Japan? They are on a remote channel way down the list of TV stations. In the one we're watching, couples have to carry each other across a field at great speed while being hotly pursued by men dressed as pink cows, carrying large green flowers which spray blue gunk. Don't ask me why we're watching it.

It's one of those shows that comes on and you think 'what's this rubbish?' but then you end up watching the whole thing, cheering on some random couple from Shirakawa-Go in Takayama, against the reigning champions from Tokyo, and genuinely wanting the underdogs to win.

'Come on Hiromasa and Gyo-Shin,' I scream. I'm up out of my seat and shouting at the television.

'You can do it,' shouts Ted.

Then some cow pats get thrown, for no obvious reason. Then they switch round so the man is being carried by the woman as they race back across the field.

'That's not hard: we could do that!' says Ted.

'No we couldn't, because we're both very heavy and I'm also very weak. If you got onto my back, I'd collapse and maybe even die.'

'No, you wouldn't, we'd be fine. We'd definitely beat this old couple from Sendai. Come on, let's try.'

I have a glass in my hand as Ted makes his ridiculous suggestion, and I'm not keen on anything that requires me to put down my glass. Ted is insistent though...he pulls me up onto my feet and drops into a deep squat, flexing his muscles like a powerlifter.

'On you get,' he says, clenching still further so the veins in his neck have popped out. It's as if he's about to lift a car or push a van down the road, like they do on *World's Strongest Man.*

'I'm not that heavy,' I say, but the groan he gives when I jump onto his back suggests otherwise. Could he not at least pretend?

'I can get to the front door,' he says, heaving and panting with the effort of it all.

'Did it!' says Ted, dropping me onto the floor in a rather undignified fashion, and running around the flat with his T-shirt over his head like Ronaldo after he scores a goal.

'I deserve some sort of award, perhaps I should become a professional weightlifter?' Then he stretches out his arms and shoulder joints like he's just done a massive workout.

'Okay, okay...' I say. 'You make it sound like you just carried a tank on your back.'

'No, of course not, angel. Sorry. I'm just being silly. Now it's your turn. You're the horse and I'm the rider. Brace yourself, I'm climbing on board.'

Ted jumps onto my back without a care for my spine, my internal organs or my knees. My legs give way immediately, and I'm sent crashing to the ground.

'I think Hiromasa and Gyo-Shin would beat us easily,' I say, as Ted helps me to my feet.

'Shall we try again?'

'For heaven sake, Ted, no. Let's not try again. Let's sit down and drink our wine, and not attempt to copy the people in the mad Japanese game show.'

'Does this mean we can't go on there, then?' Ted sounds genuinely disappointed that he won't be able to take on the good people of Sendai.

'No, not with me as your partner. Now - off you go. You need to top up my wine.' I fall back on the sofa and lift my glass to my lips, while he trundles off into the kitchen to bring me the last of the wine.

'Gosh, there's not that much left,' says Ted, returning with the drips left in the bottle and dropping them into my glass. 'Shall I open another one?'

'When, in the history of all the world, have I ever seen fit to dissuade you from opening another bottle?'

'Good point,' he says, disappearing back into the kitchen and emerging a few minutes later with a tantalisingly full bottle. He fills my glass and asks after my battered knees and breaking back.

'They're okay,' I say. 'But my back is hurting right at the bottom. It's a really dull ache. What do you think it is?'

'I don't know. What does Dr. Google say?'

I reach for my phone, preparing to list my symptoms in an effort to see what injury I may have sustained, when I see there's a pile of WhatsApp messages waiting for me.

'Someone's popular,' says Ted, who's been looking over my shoulder. 'Perhaps it's Weightlifting Today magazine, wanting to do an interview with you?'

'No, it's more exciting than that. The messages are in the Mysterious Invitation WhatsApp group.'

'The what?'

'The guys I met in Wales for the funeral. Do you remember? Raymond Charters - the guy who died and left us money.'

'Of course I remember,' says Ted. 'I didn't know you were still in touch with them.'

'No, I'm not. We set up this WhatsApp group but no one's posted in there til now.'

I read through the messages, as Ted looks over my shoulder.

'Simon's suggesting we should meet up.'

'Why?'

'We always said we would. We actually always planned to meet up and try and find the Gower family. Do you remember? They were so kind and welcoming to Reginald's dad when he came over to Wales as an Italian prisoner of war. The private detectives couldn't find them anywhere. We talked about all getting together to find them.

'Let me know if you're going to meet them. I can easily get time off.'

'Oh, you're going to come, are you? I assumed I'd just go alone. The others won't have partners with them.'

'No, I'll come.' says Ted with great certainty. 'I'd like to come along and help you.'

'Sure, well I'll reply now then, and find out what all the details are...'

'What details?' says Juan, wandering into the room with a face so bright red it looks as if he's been slapped several times across the face.

'I'm back in touch with the Mysterious Invitation people and we're planning to meet up. Ted's coming,' I explain.

'Oh wow, that sounds fun. Is there room for a little one?'

'You want to come, too?'

'Is that okay?'

'Yeah, I guess so, but I don't imagine it will be very interesting.'

'That's okay. I'll keep Ted company.'

'Right,' I say. 'Hopefully your face will have calmed down a bit by then. What on earth have you been doing to get such a bright red complexion?'

'Sirsasana,' he replies.

'Gosh, that sounds complicated.'

'It's a headstand. So, not complicated, but I held it for 40 minutes and now I feel a little odd.'

'Blimey, I'm not surprised.'

'So, when are we going?' asks Juan, joining Ted and me on the sofa and taking a huge gulp out of my glass of wine.

'I'll reply to them now, and tell them I'm in. I'll let you know.'

*Mysterious Invitation WhatsApp Group*

**Mary Brown**

Hello, it's me! How are you all? I missed all those messages because my boyfriend was trying to mount me. It didn't go well. Now my knees are sore and my back hurts!

**Mary Brown**

No, Christ. No. That sounds all wrong. When I say 'mounting me' - I mean from behind. We were copying what they were doing in this late night Japanese torture show.

**Mary Brown**

No. No, Blimey

That sounds even worse. Piggy back! He was giving me a goddamn piggyback and I tried to give him one, but I collapsed. Anyway, whatever. I wish you could delete WhatsApp messages. How are you all? Would love to catch up. Can't believe it's been a year!

**Simon Blake**

Dear Mary, You do make me laugh.

**Julie Bramley**

Me too! Let's all meet up soon.

**Matt Prior**

Oh hello everyone. And hello Mary. That was funny. If you are meeting in Wales, I'd love to come.

. . .

**Simon Blake**

I wondered whether we should meet in Llandrindod Wells? It's a delightful spa town, and it's the last-known address of Tom and Irene Gower. I'm not suggesting that we track them down or anything, but we could make a few enquiries and see where we get to? And the place is beautiful.

**Matt Prior**

Yes, I'll be there. That sounds great.

**Mike Sween**

I'll come if I can.

**Sally Bramley**

That sounds lovely. Yes, I'm in. No need for us to go trekking after the Gower family though. Let's just have a lovely weekend and catch up, and raise a glass to Reginald.

**Simon Blake**

Hear, hear!

**Mary Brown**

NO. We should totally track them down! We should do a manhunt and try to find them. Let's break into every house in

Llandrindod Wells and force them to tell us where the Gower family is. I'm going to come dressed like Miss Marple!

**Simon Blake**

Goodness. Let's meet up and see how the mood takes us. Very much looking forward to seeing you all.

**Mary Brown**

Me too. Really looking forward to seeing you and hunting the Gower family down like they're wild animals.

ff to Wales: Present Day

The day of departure has come and the three of us charge down the platform to board the train on this rather peculiar mission to join a group of people who I barely knew, in a place I've never been to, to track down a family I'd never met.

The wild ridiculousness of the situation is reflected in the sight of us: we make for the most remarkable trio, dashing along with our luggage. Juan Pablo is sporting a purple Lycra cat suit under his fake fur coat and a large hat. I set out to look comfy rather than attractive, in my warm and cosy all-in-one. It's candy-floss pink in colour, and every time I go anywhere I think it's the perfect outfit for travelling because it's all snuggly and lovely, but, also, every time I wear it I regret it instantly and wish I'd opted for something a little more sober. That applies today as well, as I run along, trying to keep up with the guys while looking like their pet teletubby.

In the front is Ted, taking the lead in his traditional, manly fashion, holding maps as if we are about to go trekking through the Andes. He is double-checking the direction of the train and the precise time it will take to get to Llandrindod Wells as if he were Indiana Jones leading us to escape from the Well of Souls.

'It's a good job I'm here,' he says, and I try ever so hard not to point out that I went off to a remote part of Wales just a year ago on this first mission to meet the mysterious invitation people, entirely alone. I did so with absolutely no problems and no maps.

'This is us,' says Ted proudly, swinging open the carriage door and standing back to allow us to step on.

'I don't know where we'd be without you,' I say.

Once we've found our seats (Ted insisted on us pre-booking), we take our places for the journey and Juan marks his territory by removing his burgundy hat and laying it gently on the coat rack above our heads.

'Tell me a little bit about these people, and what this is all about. Any hotties going?' he asks.

Juan has recently separated from his very hunky personal trainer boyfriend, and he has been like a dog on heat ever since. Honestly, I'm tempted to go to the vet to see whether I can get him neutered. Everywhere we go, he asks me whether there's anyone hot there. I don't fancy his chances in Llandrindod Wells.

'No hotties,' I tell him. 'Well, none you'd be interested in. There was a very beautiful woman called Julie who came, but she was a witch.'

'Oh good,' says Juan. 'I hope she comes. I like the idea of meeting a witch.'

'You wouldn't like her - she was icy cold and self-obsessed. She ended up not getting any of Reginald's money because we were told we had to vote for one person in the group that we liked least and she got the vote.'

'Wow - the dead guy liked to play games, didn't he?'

'Big time. I mean, the whole funeral was full of these odd things he did based on the plays he'd written. It was all so surreal. Julie was really fed up but the rest of us were quietly delighted. She had a sister called Sally who was nice. I liked her. I hope she comes this weekend. She was very kind and good company.'

'Tell me about the others,' says Juan, leaning over toward me. 'I never realised this funeral was such a riot. They sound like characters from a Victorian novel. We've got the glamorous, feuding sisters. What other glamorous lovelies were there?'

'The others were all men,' I say. Ted makes a strange snorting sound of disapproval.

'What was that noise for?'

'I didn't realise you'd been gallivanting all over the place with a bunch of men.'

'I'm not sure that going to a funeral qualifies as gallivanting.'

'Carry on, darling,' says Juan.

'So there was Matt Prior - a young Welsh guy. I'm not sure whether he's coming or not. He was a good looking boy - only around 20-years-old but a real sweetheart. Then there was Mike Sween who was quite good-looking and always smartly dressed, works for SKY, I think.'

The truth is that Mike Sween is bloody gorgeous, but if I say that to Ted, given the mood he's in, he'll start whimpering and moaning.

'Then the final person to mention is Simon. He was like the leader of the group, really, because he's older and seemed that much more grown up and sensible than the rest of us. I liked him a lot.'

'The leader? You never mentioned him before. How big is he?' interrupts Ted. I glance at Juan and he shakes his head, as if to advise me not to engage; not to argue with him.

'And that's all?' Juan says. 'I thought there were more of you than that?'

'Nope. Just the six of us...all sitting in a room at this old farm house that had been turned into a hotel, wondering why on earth we were there at all. Of course, there should have been someone from the Gower family as well.

'I had a strong feeling that it was Tom and Irene Gower who Reginald felt he owed the most to, because of the kindness they had shown to his father when he came over in the war. But the private detectives never tracked them down. Apparently they tried everything but there was no sight of them anywhere.'

'It's so weird. I thought it was possible to track anyone down.'

'I don't think they had enough time. They only had a week or so to find all of us. If the Gowers had moved abroad, it would have taken much longer.'

'Presumably the private detectives carried on looking for them?'

'No. You'd think they would have, but I called them yesterday and was told that Paul - the guy who owns the agency - has been very ill so nothing's happened. There is a lot of money sitting there for them. I'd love us to go on a mission to find them.'

By the time we arrive in Llandrindod Wells it's almost 6pm. It's a cold, sharp winter's night, and the scene that greets us outside the station is picture postcard perfect: sparkling lights illuminating a village green. Even in the semi-darkness, you can see how beautiful the place is: with lovely dry stone walls, lots of trees and bars and restaurants scattered around, all lit by these elegant, old-fashioned street lamps that look as if they've been lifted out of the Edwardian era. It's no wonder the Gower family moved here. It's lovely.

'This place gives me the creeps,' says Juan, pulling his massive fur coat tightly round him. Juan is so incredibly slim, and the coat so large that he looks like he's being eaten by an enormous bear when he does that.

'The creeps? I think it's lovely.'

'It's just so twee. Like the opening scene from a detective series. You know - the lovely, pretty town where nothing goes wrong, then suddenly - bam! Everyone is found murdered.'

'Well, I really hope not,' I say, glancing over at Ted who is too engrossed in the map to join in our debate about whether this place is lovely or Wales' answer to *Midsomer Murders*. I half expect him to pull out a head torch and a compass. Then he lifts his head up and points straight ahead.

'There,' he says, his finger stretched out toward the hotel ahead. 'That's where we're staying.' There's huge pride in his voice, as he nods and smiles to himself.

'Thanks for getting us here safely,' I say, magnanimously.

'Safe for now,' says Juan. 'Until we are brutally murdered in our beds by the vicar clutching a bell rope.'

'Come on, you nutter, let's go and check in then we can get ourselves a drink.'

'A drink from the poisoned well,' says Juan.

The hotel is very swish, much posher than I thought it would be. The place I stayed when I came to Wales for the funeral was little more than a farmhouse that had been converted into a simple, country B&B, and I suppose I had expected much the same thing, but this place is a proper hotel, with people in uniforms and a fancy reception desk. There are signs around the place indicating where the restaurants and bars are, and which way to go for the spa, gym and the swimming pool.

'Ohhh,' I say, pointing at the sign for the swimming pool, and giving Juan a hug.

I have a rather odd relationship with exercise in hotels. It always strikes me as a really good idea. Half the problem with going to the gym or to the swimming pool is being bothered to go there in the first place. The thought of getting on the bus, getting there, getting changed, exercising, then showering, getting changed and back on the bus again - I mean, who can be bothered with all that faffing around? But hotels seem like a very civilized place in which to exercise because the facilities are right there - down the corridor. It's like having a gym and pool in your own house.

But—and this is quite a big but—hotels also have bars in them, and restaurants, and room service. And a room with a huge bed with a big television in front of it. Now who, in the name of all that is holy, would rather go to the gym than lie on the bed and watch *This Morning*, while a nice man in a smart uniform knocks on the door and hands you the large cheese-burger you ordered? And all of the ordering and TV watching can be done from bed.

So, the long and the short of it is that I always take my swimming costume when I go to a hotel because it's a lovely idea, but I've never yet used a hotel pool because room service is a better idea.

We walk across the lobby, toward the reception desk, when Juan spots someone and his interest is immediately piqued.

'Oh hello - here's someone who bats for my team,' he says, letting his enormous coat swing open and pouting off into the distance.

The man he's staring at is tall, neatly-dressed and bending over to pick up his bag.

'How on earth can you tell from this distance when the guy's facing away from us?'

'If you know, you know...'

The man moves away from the reception desk and turns round, then he walks toward us.

'Told you,' says Juan.

'Hello Mary, how lovely to see you,' says the man.

'Simon, my goodness, this is good timing. How are you?'

'Very well.'

I can see Juan's eyes light up in disbelief that I know the guy.

'This is Juan, a very good friend of mine,' I say.

'Charmed, I'm sure,' says Juan with a sort of leg bend, like a mini-curtsey. He says his peculiar greeting in such an odd voice that Ted and I both stare at him in alarm.

'This is Ted, my boyfriend,' I say.

Ted offers a much more normal: 'nice to meet you' and the two men shake hands.

Simon doesn't look gay to me. Why the hell did does Juan think he's gay?

'I didn't know you were bringing anyone,' says Simon. 'I regret to say that I came alone.'

'Oh, Ted and Juan just fancied a few days away, so it made sense for them to come,' I say, almost apologetically.

'No - it's great. And you've just enhanced our numbers. It seems that you and I are the only people coming here.'

'Really? Oh. I thought we were going to have a proper one year reunion.'

'Well, yes, that's exactly what I thought, too. I reserved a load of rooms, and have just had to unreserve them. Still, it's very lovely to see you, Mary, and to meet your friends. Do you fancy dinner tonight? We should make the most of our time here...it's a very beautiful place. We could meet in the restaurant downstairs at eight? It's supposed to be very good.'

'Or at seven?' I venture. I'm starving already. If I'm forced to wait until 8pm, I'll empty the mini bar.

'Oh right. Yes, that's not a bad idea. You're probably hungry after travelling all day. An early supper it is, then. I'll book for four of us, shall I? In Mezzet, just through there.'

We all follow Simon's finger as he points to the restaurant nestled in the corner, to the left of the reception desk.

'Perfect. See you there in an hour.'

'I feel a fool now,' says Ted. 'I thought there was a huge big group going. Now I know it's only the two of you, it feels idiotic that we're all here.'

'No it doesn't, if I'd come back and told you that it was just Simon and me, you'd have accused me of all sorts of things. Anyway, some of the others might decide to come out tomorrow, you never know.'

I hope they do. I'd like to see Sally again, and obviously it would be rather lovely to get an eyeful of Mighty Mike the Magnificent Stud (that's his official title, but I call him Mike, for short).

Seven o'clock takes a long time to appear. Ted snoozes while I wander round the bedroom, picking things up and putting them back down again while sighing loudly. It's because I'm hungry: hunger has the ability to turn me into a recalcitrant-teenager as soon as it bites.

I'm exactly the same at work: five minutes can take three hours to roll past when we're heading toward lunchtime. I'll stand at my till at 12.30pm, unsure whether I'm going to make it to my 1pm lunch-break because I'm so hungry I can barely breathe. Then I'll serve someone, chat to them, help them take their purchases to the car, and think - right it must be lunchtime now. When I get back to the till it's 12.32. What? That can't be right. Usain Bolt couldn't have done it that quickly. I think the clocks are messing with my head. Clocks are evil. I might try to get a grant to do an investigation into my clock theory.

Anyway - sorry, I got a bit distracted there. The thing is that time drags when I'm hungry. I have spent ages unpacking and hanging everything up neatly in the wardrobe with those hangers that don't actually come out, so you have to hang the clothes on them while they're still attached to the rail which involves virtually climbing into the wardrobe. Then I got ready nicely and did my makeup so I looked as good as possible. Then finally, finally, the clock deigns to tell me that it is time for food, so Ted and I head downstairs.

'What did you do while I was sleeping?' asks Ted.

'Mainly worked on my thesis about clocks.'

'What thesis is this?' he asks.

'That they are evil.'

'Sure,' he says, and I find myself smiling to myself. It's joyous to be with a man who can cope with all my eccentricities. I mean - how many guys would say 'sure' when I shared my view that clocks are evil?

We're first to arrive at the restaurant, so we take our seats and order drinks and some nibbles (before I DIE of hunger).

Around ten minutes later, Juan and Simon arrive - together. TOGETHER.

'Oh God, what fresh hell is this?' I mutter to Ted, as Simon courteously pulls out a chair for Juan, and my lovely Spanish friend slips into it, fanning his face with his fingers like Marlene Dietrich.

'We met in the lobby just now,' says Simon, perhaps sensing the inaccurate conclusion I was drifting toward.

'Of course,' I reply, as if I were the sort of person who would ever entertain such a conclusion.

It turns out that Mezzet is the most beautiful restaurant. I can't quite believe how tasty all the food is. We have a mosaic of colourful starters in the middle of the table: hummus, vine leaves, tabbouleh, these insanely tasty chargrilled chicken pieces and all sorts of other gorgeous Lebanese bits. Then big salads arrive and baskets of pita bread. It is fantastic, and I have to stop myself from shoving everything into my mouth at record-breaking speed as I try to enjoy all the flavours at once.

I eat so much that I'm ready to burst, then Simon says: 'Remember - these are only the starters.'

And I wish I wasn't so insanely greedy. The main courses are a triumph of flavours and size. I have chicken coated in this gorgeous, spicy garlicky flavouring that comes with a lovely Greek salad, and the heftiest portion of chips you've ever seen.

They've left some of the dips on the table, so I show just how suave and sophisticated I am by dipping the chips into hummus and tzatziki, while wolfing it all down with glasses of lovely oaky Chardonnay. My favourite.

Most of the talking over dinner is done by Ted and Simon who appear to share a love of map reading and geography.

'No, it's just off the A47, before you get to Norwich...'

'Oh, I know,' says Ted. 'There's a service station there, isn't there?'

Oh my goodness. I try to smile and nod in the right places, but Juan has stopped even trying. He looks like a bored schoolboy as he checks his phone, looks around the restaurant, and slumps further into his seat.

'Are you going to go and look for the Gower family tomorrow?' Juan asks, when he spots me looking at him.

'Probably not,' says Simon, before I've had time to answer.

'Oh. Mary said she thought it would be a good idea. Since we're here.'

'It feels slightly odd to bother: we know they're not there. If they were there, the private detectives would have found them and given them the money.'

'I don't think the private detectives have been looking for them at all since the funeral. Paul Dillon, the main guy, is really ill, apparently. I think it's worth us trying to find them.

'I mean, I know they aren't there now, but we might be able to find out where they went? We could pop along to the address you've got tomorrow. After breakfast?'

Simon is silent as he seems to be weighing up the options. This is something I never do: if I weighed up the options and thought about the consequences once in a while I'd have had a very different life.

'Maybe we could find out if there's anyone in the area who knew them or was around when they lived here. For the sake of an hour out of our day when we've got nothing else planned. Why not?' I add.

'Okay,' says Simon. 'Yes, you're right: we're here, let's go round there in the morning.'

'Can I come?' asks Juan, suddenly awake and back in the room with us.

'Yes, we'll all go,' I say, before Simon can suggest otherwise.

'Let's head there after breakfast,' he says. 'The house is in a little village a short walk from here. The house is called Home Sweet Home.'

# CHAPTER 3

## $\mathcal{W}$ ales: 1960

The door to 'Home Sweet Home' was wide open. Tom sat back in the big floral armchair that had been in the family since he was a boy and lifted his feet onto the stool in front of him. He lay his head back and closed his eyes, determined to rest after moving boxes all morning. The breeze from outside wafted in, cooling him down, but he still felt like he was overheating after the exhaustion of all that packing. Irene hummed to herself while she made a pot of tea in the kitchen, and from upstairs came the sound of loud music and banging as his son, Tom Junior, packed up all his things.

'There you go, my love: a cup of tea and a couple of biscuits,' said Irene, putting the tray down on the coffee table in front of him. 'What's the door doing open? Shall I shut it?'

'No, leave it open. I like the breeze, and Tom's mates will be here in a minute to help bring the furniture down from upstairs. Have a sit down.'

Irene collapsed into the chair next to him. She looked tired. She was only 45-years-old and had always been exceptionally beautiful, with perfect skin and such delicate features, but today she looked drained. Her complexion had assumed the unattractive pallor of the pale china ornaments staring out at him from the box by his feet. Moving house was a hideous business.

'I'm looking forward to moving, and starting a new job. But let's never move again. You look exhausted, love.'

'I am tired. You know: it's not too late to change your mind. We could stay here. We don't have to move,' she replied.

Irene smiled at her husband as she spoke, but he didn't smile back. They had developed very different views about Llandrindod Wells, the place they'd called home for over a decade.

She had no desire to move from this lovely area, teeming with glorious countryside, but with an urban heart. There were restaurants aplenty and bars that felt modern and fun. It was a place that felt like home: not like Gower where it was all about farming: morning, noon and night. Irene had never enjoyed their life in farming. She had tolerated it because Tom loved it so much, but it had never been something she enjoyed.

She had made Tom move from Gower and across the country so she could be near her parents when her son was young. They'd settled here, in Llandrindod, a place where there was life and laughter. Irene adored it; she saw people every day, loved the local boutiques and had more friends than she'd known in her life before.

Tom had just tolerated it, in the same way as she had tolerated their time on the farm. Now Tom had been offered a job back in the world of farming and she needed to move to the south coast of England with him. It would have been unfair of her to refuse him the chance to take an exciting new job that took him back into the world of farming and farmers, even though every fibre of her yearned to stay where they were, in their lovely house, in this beautiful place.

Tom smiled warmly at his wife as he sipped his tea. He was looking forward to moving, and it wasn't fair of Irene to keep telling him how much she wanted to stay. They had been in Llandrindod Wells for so long. It had been the perfect place in which to bring up young Tom after they left the farm, but it wasn't home; not like Gower had been. He'd never quite fitted in the way he hoped he would.

Giving up farming and starting a new way had been a mistake. He'd realised that almost straight away. He was a farmer, and a farmer's son, and farming was all he had ever known. Now, at the ripe old age of 47, he had a chance to go back to it. Well, not quite back to hands-on farming...he wouldn't be up at 4am to milk cows, and return with mud under his fingernails after a long day in the fields, but he would be back in that world. He'd been offered a job as an agricultural expert at Portsmouth University, where the new degree in land management involved an option called farming studies and farm management. And he —Tom Gower—was going to be teaching them.

A noise outside indicated the arrival of Llyr and Richard; Tom Junior's closest friends.

'The heavy mob have arrived,' said Llyr, popping his head round the door. 'Can we come in, Professor Gower?'

'Very funny,' said Tom. 'I'm not quite a professor.'

'Come in, you clowns,' said Irene, jumping up and hugging

them warmly. The boys blushed as she did so. She was by far the better looking of all the mothers: a lovely face, stunning figure, and always dressed so beautifully.

'You've timed it well, the kettle just boiled. Have a seat and I'll call Tom down.'

'No, don't you worry,' said Richard. 'We'll head up and help him to bring all the furniture down, then we'll stop for tea, if that's okay?'

'Good idea,' said Tom Senior. 'You youngsters get up there and do the heavy lifting. Shout if you need any help from me.'

'No, we'll be okay, grandad, you're too old for this sort of work,' said Llyr.

'He's a cheeky sod,' muttered Tom.

'You'll miss those guys when we move away,' said Irene. 'They've been good friends to all of us.'

Tom nodded. He refused to feel guilty about the move. He had felt awful when he first accepted it, of course. He was even concerned that she might not come with him. He was also worried that his son wouldn't want to come. But Tom Junior, or TJ as he was known to everyone, had taken the news well. In fact, TJ thought it was a great idea. He had been quietly despairing of the job situation in Wales, after returning from university in Gloucester, and saw it as a sign that he too should be in England, and he immediately began applying for jobs in the south, sending off letters for every available management position in every department in the council. His persistence paid off, and before too long he had landed himself a junior management role. So the whole family would move down to the south of England for a totally new life.

'Penny for them,' said Irene as she moved to tape up one of the many boxes lying on the ground in front of them.

'Oh nothing. Just thinking how lucky we are. It's great that TJ is coming with us, and so good that he's found himself a job he likes. It seems strange that this time next week he'll be heading out to work every morning as a manager.'

'I'm very proud of him,' said Irene.

'Me too,' said Tom. 'Very proud. And great that he starts straight away. I'm going to be hanging around for a month before I start...I just want to get going.'

'What do you mean? You'll be spending time with me, and helping me to sort the house out.'

'Yes, yes. Of course - will be lovely.'

Irene looked unsure.

'It's all going to be okay, you know.'

She nodded gently without commenting.

'I love you,' said Tom.

'I love you, too.' Irene stood up and surveyed the boxes all around. She was determined to keep active so she didn't have time to think too much about everything...like the lovely life, friends and job she was leaving behind. Being active would keep her sane.

'So, the question now is - why, oh why, did you let me accumulate so much stuff? Have you seen how much is here? I've already thrown away everything that hasn't been used for years, and taken bags of old clothes to the charity shop. And there's still a ton left.'

Irene pulled the nearest box toward her and glanced inside it.

'Do you think we should take all this stuff? Or just chuck a load more. Oh - look....'

Irene pulled out two photo albums, some newspaper

cuttings and various notes and papers from TJ's school when he was young.

'Look at this picture of a dinosaur,' said Irene, holding up the brightly painted picture so Tom could see it.

TJ and his friends descended the stairs as she held the magnificent artwork aloft.

'Actually Mam, that was a picture of Dad. Didn't he have blue overalls like those in the picture that he wore on the farm?'

'Yes he did.'

'But why have I got a horn on my face?' asked Tom.

'I think that's supposed to be your nose. You do have a huge hooter, Da.'

The boys joined them as Irene opened one of the photo albums and flicked through it.

'Look at you,' she said to TJ. The picture was of a young boy standing in a field with a handsome young Italian man.

'Marco,' said Irene quietly, looking at her husband. 'That was May 7th, 1945. The day the war was over. We asked Marco to move in with us and live on the farm that day. He was such a lovely guy. So gentle and kind, and such a hard worker. He doted on you, TJ.'

'I remember him,' said Tom Junior. 'Only vaguely, but I do remember. Didn't he make us ice cream once, or something like that?'

'Yes, he did. We gave him some time off and we came back to find that instead of relaxing, he'd prepared all this beautiful Italian ice cream for us. I wish we'd kept in touch. It was crazy not to stay in contact.'

'Have you not heard anything from him recently?'

'No, not at all. I know they were having a lot of trouble with their son. He was quite a sickly child, and never went out. They withdrew during that time. It was very difficult for them. I sent a card and a letter but never heard back. I guess with all the ice cream parlours opening, and the child being hard work, they just didn't have the time to respond. The boy must be around five or six now, I guess. His name was Joe, wasn't it? The same as Marco's grandfather, and all the ice cream shops were named after him. I hope she's having an easier time of it.'

'You should track them down, love. If the ice cream shops are still going, someone there must know what happened to Marco.'

'Yes, you know, I think I will. Once we get to Southsea and get ourselves settled, I'll see whether I can find an address for them and drop them a line. Oh, look. See what we have here.'

Irene pulled out piles of drawings done by Tom Senior. 'I remember you doing all these. I'm so pleased that we still have them.'

'They're brilliant,' said Llyr, descending the stairs ahead of the others. 'Did you really do them, Tom? I didn't know you were an artist?'

The pictures were cartoonish in style, depicting the animals on the farm, and many of them featuring TJ.

'I used to love drawing, I did it whenever I could. I might try and get back to it when we're settled in Southsea.'

'I hate to say anything nice to you, Mr Gower, but these are very good. You should definitely do some more.'

'Yes, I will. Now, you guys, shall we get everything packed up and into the hallway ready for the removal van in the morning, then we can relax and have some tea and cake.'

'Yes boss,' chorused the boys as they dragged, lifted, pulled and pushed the boxes containing the lives of the Gower family until they were all piled up by the front door.

## CHAPTER 4

# $\mathcal{A}$ new beginning: 1960

'Are you nervous?' asked Irene, as she watched her husband get ready for work. She was used to seeing him in overalls in the mornings: clean when he left the house and laced with oil, mud and dirt when he returned. He'd been doing manual jobs in Llandrindod Wells. Now here he was, preparing to go to work at a university, all dressed up in a shirt and tie. Irene swept her hand across the shoulder of his jacket. There was no fluff to remove, but she wanted him to feel looked after, and as if he were as clean and presentable as possible.

'I'm terrified,' he said. 'This is a university, for goodness sake. No one in my family has ever been to university, let alone got a job in one. What if I'm useless?'

'You won't be. You're going to be brilliant,' she said. And she knew he would be. The two of them had had some difficulties in their marriage because they were very different people, but his abilities and expertise in farming were beyond debate. He'd be great, and love the new job. But she could tell that he wasn't as convinced, and she could see, by the set of his jaw, that he was clenching his teeth with nerves.

'I'll see you tonight, okay?' he said.

'Yes, love. Good luck today. Remember that TJ is bringing Yvonne round later. He wants us to meet her.'

'TJ and his women. How many of them have we met now? And does he really need to bring her round tonight?'

'It's the first girl he's met since we've been down here. He seems to be taking it seriously.'

'Seriously? He's only known her a few weeks.'

'I know, but he likes her. I think this one's different. He seems properly smitten.'

'Okay, okay. I'll see you later.'

Irene stood at the window and watched her husband's back disappear from view.

'He'll be fine,' said TJ, running down the stairs and past the boxes to stand next to her at the window. TJ had been working at his new job for a few weeks now, and seemed to be faring admirably: they had commended him at work, he'd met new friends and had even bagged himself a girlfriend. Such was the power of youth that he had slipped into life on the south coast without a backward glance.

It had been different for Irene. She felt lonely and so far away from everyone she loved. She felt like she had no purpose, no point. She rang her friends every day and listened enviously as they spoke of meeting for coffee and how they missed her.

'If I can cope with all the changes, so can Dad,' said TJ,

assuming that his mother had gone quiet because she was worrying about her husband.

'You're tougher than your father,' she said. 'He's a gentle, sensitive soul. I hope he'll be okay.'

'He will,' said TJ, kissing his mother's head. 'I promise you. It's a five minute walk to work, and when he gets there he'll be talking about farming all day; the thing he loves most in the world: way more than he loves us. You wait, he'll be buzzing by the time he gets home. Now, are you coming to the station with me?'

Irene had fallen into the habit of walking to the station with TJ in the morning to get some exercise and fresh air before returning to the house to open more boxes, and hunt for a job. She was keen to contribute to the household. They weren't desperate for money. TJ was contributing to the rent and Tom's income was better than anything he'd earned previously, but things were so expensive here, much more so than anywhere they'd lived previously. She also thought it would be good for her, mentally, to be out working, and to feel like she was worth something. She didn't want to descend into emotional darkness like she had before. If it hadn't been for the lively spirit of Marco on the farm, she knew she'd have found the life there, particularly during the war, impossible to deal with.

As she and TJ walked along the seafront, she made herself stop thinking and worrying, and pushed herself to enjoy the feeling of the warm spring breeze ruffling her hair. The water glistened to one side of her, as the morning sunshine played across the sea, glinting and sparkling. On the other side, she looked at the big houses and hotels where people were beginning to wake up and face the day. Irene had always enjoyed early mornings. Even the crazily early alarms they had endured when they were on the farm hadn't bothered her. She hadn't enjoyed farming much, but she'd been fine with the early mornings. She was more alive first thing than at any other time.

Along the promenade they passed dog walkers who nodded and bid them good morning. Out to sea they could see swimmers enjoying a refreshing start to the day. Irene glanced at them with envy. There seemed to be something so earthy and natural about an early morning swim. She'd love to come down one day and join them, but knew she'd never have the confidence, or be brave enough to swim by herself.

'Here we are, then,' said TJ, as they approached the train station. 'Remember that Yvonne is coming over tonight. I think you'll really like her.'

'Don't worry, I haven't forgotten. I'll buy a nice chicken and roast it later. Have a lovely day,' she said to her son, feeling a flutter of sadness as he strode off to catch the train.

# CHAPTER 5

# ℳaking a Mark:1960

Irene had so much to do that she wouldn't get bored, but she'd begun to feel lonely on the walk back home from the train station. She missed having people to talk to, and neighbours to call on. She missed seeing friendly faces everywhere. She missed the sense of community that living in a small town for a long time can bring. She felt selfish and unreasonable. She had so much: she should be glad that she was healthy and had a kind husband and wonderful son instead of constantly feeling miserable.

Irene sat down on a bench on the seafront and looked out at the dots in the waves: it was the early morning swimmers she'd been watching earlier. Was there some sort of club? she wondered. There was a small wooden hut on the seafront with towels discarded outside it. Presumably they belonged to the swimmers in the sea. Perhaps that was where they congregated first thing, before hitting the waves. She stood up to go over and find out whether there was anyone in there who could assist her.

'Oh. Was it something I said?'

Irene turned around to see a handsome man had joined her on the other end of the bench. He was mid-50s, at a guess, with lovely, thick, salt and pepper hair which gave him the aura of a fading film star. He was smartly dressed as if he were heading off to work, with a briefcase at his feet.

'I didn't mean to startle you. I just saw a beautiful woman, sitting alone on the bench, looking out to sea, and I thought I'd join her. But the minute I sat down, the lady stood up.'

'Ha. Nothing personal, I assure you,' said Irene. 'I was watching the swimmers and thought I might head over there and find out a bit more about them and how often they meet,' she said.

'I'll come with you,' said the man. 'I'm Mark, by the way.'

She felt slightly wary of him as she shook hands with the stranger, and felt herself colour as he smiled at her. He was dripping with confidence and bravado. But he had such a nice smile, a kind smile. And it was so nice to talk to someone new.

'Do you live near here?' she asked.

Mark turned and pointed at one of the gorgeous big houses on the seafront. 'Right there,' he said. 'I haven't had to travel far this morning.'

She smiled. 'What a beautiful home. And how lovely to be able to see the sea from the windows. Have you lived there long?'

He shook his head gently. She sensed in him a reluctance to

talk about himself, a reluctance which in turn sparked a desire in her to know all about him.

'Where were you before?' she asked.

'Come on,' he said, leading her over to the hut. 'Let's see who's here. There must be someone here who can tell us all about early morning sea swimming.'

She followed him down the stone steps to the beach and over to where the hut sat, in splendid isolation, accompanied only by the discarded towels of the morning swimmers.

As they neared the small, wooden shed, they saw that it was locked with a rusty padlock that bore the ravages of time.

'Well no one's been in here for a while. Perhaps there's no club. It might just be where they drop their towels,' said Irene.

'Only one way to find out. We'll wait until some of them get out of the water and ask them. I could get us a couple of coffees if you want to wait? We could watch the waves for a while, then talk to the swimmers.'

She had so much to do: unpacking and searching for a job, getting the house ready for Yvonne's visit, preparing and cooking dinner. But the pull of the ocean and this gentle man's company drew her to nod and say that she'd like to stay.

Irene headed to the bench to wait, while Mark rushed off to get them both coffees, returning with take-away cups from the café further down the seafront.

Irene wasn't a huge fan of coffee; she much preferred tea, but he'd offered coffee, and it seemed far more sophisticated than boring old tea, so she sat with it warming her hands, blowing across the dark liquid occasionally and chatting to her new friend.

She told Mark about her husband and son, and how they'd only just moved down from Wales, and she didn't really know anyone. She explained that she was looking for a job – just basic secretarial work – while she found her feet and got to know more people in the area.

Then she asked about him.

'I've lived in Southsea all my life. I own Grants Estate Agents in Old Portsmouth,' he said. 'There's not much else to know.'

'Do you have a family? Children?' she asked.

He looked down.

'I met Amanda, fell in love, and got married. We bought that beautiful big house on the seafront. Life was wonderful. She died. That's my family story.'

Irene gasped and leaned over to touch his arm. 'I'm so sorry.'

Mark just nodded. 'Look I probably should get to work. Fancy swimming in the morning?'

'I'm not a strong enough swimmer to go out there by myself,' said Irene. 'I love swimming but...'

'Then why don't I come with you? I'll meet you here at 7am and we'll have our first sea swim. What do you think?'

'We could do,' said Irene. 'Were you going to come anyway?'

'If you're coming, I'll come.'

'7am?'

'Yes.'

'We'll meet here?'

'Yes,' he said. 'By this hut.'

'Okay. Yes, that would be great. See you then.'

Irene watched Mark as he walked away, raising his arm above his head to bid her goodbye without turning round or breaking his stride.

Irene put down the paper cup full of coffee. The smell of it was so strong and the prospect of its bitterness so overwhelming, there was no way she could drink it. She should have asked for tea. Why did she ask for coffee in order to seem cool? What an idiot.

Irene walked back home and worked her way through the list of chores that her afternoon presented her with. But as she stood in a queue in the butchers, picked the nicest vegetables in the greengrocers and looked longingly at the lovely spring outfits that had appeared in the little clothes shop, she couldn't stop thinking about Mark.

There were so many unanswered questions.

He lost his wife. Poor guy. He couldn't be more than 40-years-old. How did she die? When did she die?

Irene pushed the chicken into the oven and set the timer, then she moved the unopened boxes to the room under the stairs so the sitting room looked as warm and welcoming as possible. She'd promised herself that she wouldn't do that. Most of the boxes were open now and if she left the unopened ones out in the middle of the room, in plain sight, she'd be forced to open them and sort out the contents. By tucking them away she'd be tempted to ignore them for months. But TJ's new girl-friend was coming, so away they went, shoved in and piled high alongside the hoover, the broom and their rickety old ironing board.

While the smell of chicken filtered out of the kitchen and through the house, Irene flicked through the local paper looking for job ads. But her mind wasn't on the task. She thought mainly of Mark. How on earth was he coping without his wife? Did they have children? He hadn't mentioned children. He'd been through so much.

There was a reprieve from the tumble of thoughts when TJ came back from work, throwing himself into the house at 3pm after a half-day in the office.

'Day off tomorrow. Yeeeeees!' he said, pulling her in close to him to give her a big hug.

'You look nice,' he said, gently touching her hair.

'Oh, thank you.'

She'd tried something a bit different with her hair. No reason. She just thought it might be time for a change. She'd also hitched her skirt up a little, to make it look more modern. Young women were wearing their skirts so short these days.

'What have you been up to today?'

'Oh you know – this and that. I met some people on the seafront and I'm going swimming with them tomorrow morning.'

'You look love-struck,' said TJ. 'Like you're a teenage girl who kissed a boy for the first time.'

'What on earth is that supposed to mean?'

'Oh – nothing – just you, talking about swimming, you look happy. It's a good thing, Mum. Don't snap at me.'

'Oh right. Well, get yourself changed and ready for when Yvonne comes round.'

'Sure,' he said, hugging her again, and wondering why she'd suddenly turned so frosty. He was pleased that she wanted to go swimming in the mornings. Christ, women were so complicated.

At 5pm, Tom came home from work earlier than expected, shouting news of his return through the house, as if he were returning victorious from battle. 'Hello, hello, something smells delicious,' he said as he strode into the kitchen, full of joy and happiness.

'You seem pleased. Did it all go well?'

'Great,' he said, with a beaming smile. 'It was really good to be talking about farming again. You know some of those people running the course have never worked as farmers? They know nothing about farming. Their advice to the students and their notes for the students were all wrong. Well, no – not wrong – just very theoretical, you know. Farming doesn't actually work that way. I'm going to advise them on practical farming methods. I mean, I know there's a difference between the theory and the practical, but there's no point in teaching theoretical farming that bears no resemblance to the realities of running a farm, is there?'

'No,' said, Irene. She pulled the sizzling chicken out of the oven and placed it gently on the side, hoping her husband might come over and start to carve it, then she removed the roast potatoes and lifted the giant pan of vegetables off the stove. The thing was so heavy, it hurt her arms to lift it. She gave a small groan, but Tom didn't notice. Then she collected the meat juices to stir into the gravy.

Tom sat down at the kitchen table. 'I think I'm going to make a success of this. It's great to be excited about something for a change. It reminds me of when we set up the ice-cream shop at the farm, for Marco to run. Do you remember? It was a really exciting time because it was new and it was all about us and our skills. Now I've got the chance to use my skills to teach people properly about farming. Not just from books and notes on the blackboard, but from me – someone who grew up on a farm and knows what it took.'

'I had a nice day, too,' said Irene, not waiting to be asked, as she moved everything off the table in order to lay it for dinner. Why couldn't Tom help with this, instead of leaving it all up to her? 'I sat down by the seafront and ended up chatting to some people who go on morning swims. I'm going to go and join them tomorrow. They are meeting at 7am for a swim in the sea.'

It was just a small lie. Barely a lie at all. She'd said 'some people' when it was 'one man', that was all.

'What? You're going to go swimming in the sea first thing in the morning?'

'Tom, it's something I've always fancied doing, and there's a group of them, so I'll be quite safe.'

'Well, make sure you're quiet when you get up. I've got a busy day tomorrow. Oh, and I won't be back til late. There's a 'get to know the staff' evening for the freshers that I need to go to. It's going to be strange, but wonderful, getting into college life. They seem like such a nice bunch. I'm looking forward to meeting them all properly tomorrow.'

'Oh, right. What time do you think you'll be back?'

'No idea,' said Tom. 'Difficult to tell. Why, is it a problem?'

'No, not a problem, it's just that I don't really know anyone.'

'You'll get to know people in no time. The swimmers – they might be good fun?'

'Yes, yes. I'll be fine. Could you call TJ and Yvonne and tell them dinner's ready?'

'Yvonne's here already?'

'Yes –in the sitting room. I assumed that you'd spoken to them when you came in.'

'No. I didn't realise there was anyone in there. Are they in there with all the mess and unopened boxes?'

'No, I tidied them away, Tom.'

'I wish you'd said that she was here. I'd have gone in to talk to them.'

'You can talk to her over dinner. She's lovely.'

'Who is?'

'Yvonne – TJ's girlfriend. The woman we were just talking about. She's a real sweetheart.'

'Oh good, good. I'll go and wash my hands and call them in then. Isn't it great that everything's going so well?'

'It's wonderful, Tom. I'm really pleased.'

The evening passed in a warm glow of friendship and harmony, as Yvonne told them all about her life, growing up in Brighton, further down the coast. She'd moved to Southsea just a year ago, with her older sister, and she worked as a nurse at Portsmouth General.

Irene was delighted. Yvonne had that kind and gentle disposition that one so readily associates with those in the nursing profession. She was down to earth, sensible and seemed loyal and keen to show how much she adored Irene's only son.

'You're right. She's lovely,' said Tom when the two youngsters had retired to the sitting room, leaving Irene and Tom alone among the detritus of the evening meal. 'I like her. They're a good match.'

'I agree. I hope they make a go of this. It would be nice for him to find someone to settle down with. I know he's only young but it means they can take their time and build the courtship and get to know each other properly.'

Tom gave his wife a hug. 'I'm going to read through some notes, and get an early night before college tomorrow. I'll suggest that TJ walks Yvonne home now. You need to get an early night too, if you're swimming tomorrow.'

'I've got a lot of tidying up to do first,' she said, but Tom had left the room. She heard him talking to TJ as she plunged her hands into the lukewarm soapy water. There was never enough hot water. There were always too many dirty dishes. She was glad she was going swimming in the sea.

. . .

Morning came abruptly: the sharp cold of the ocean clashing with the gentle lightness of the emerging sun. Mark swam fearlessly: around her, under her and across her as she laughed, splashed and felt a freedom and delight at being out and about, and with someone who seemed thrilled in her company. There was something both understated and flamboyant about taking to the seas in the morning, while others still slept. It was the most natural thing in the world to do, yet somehow decadent and wonderful to splash through this narrow stretch of the Atlantic Ocean. She squealed with joy and dived down under the water, only to be pulled back up by Mark.

'You are wonderful,' he shouted across the waves as she lifted her head to face the cracks of early morning sunshine breaking through the quiet skies. His words didn't seem frightening or inappropriate or anything. Just wonderful. Then the cold gripped her, forcing her to swim faster, then sprint out across the beach to her towel.

'You okay?' asked Mark, touching her nose gently with the tip of his finger, a move so warm and sincere that it brought tears to her eyes.

On the bench on the seafront, looking out at them, also with tears in his eyes, was her son, Tom Junior.

# CHAPTER 6

$\mathcal{W}$ales: Present Day

'Hello, hello,' I shout through the front door of *Home Sweet Home*, expecting to see a farmer and his wife standing there, looking exactly like the picture we have of the Gower family from about thirty years ago.

Instead, I am confronted by two girls in their early twenties gleefully sipping some blue drink, possibly 'Wkd', and listening to music that is so loud they have to scream at one another to be heard.

'I don't think that's Tom Gower,' I say to Simon.

'Possibly not. No blue dungarees.'

'Come in, come in, we are ready for you,' shouts the blonde girl. She has so many earrings decorating her lobes that they have disappeared up her ear and into her mane of bleached blonde hair. If the colour doesn't give away the fact that her hair is dyed, the jet black line at her hairline certainly does. I'm not being critical: every woman who has had highlights knows all about that evil line that appears at the roots. I'm just painting a picture for you, so you know what we're dealing with here.

'You're ready for me? That's wonderful. I'm Mary. How did you know I was coming?'

The two girls look at each other and pull a face which suggests they think the woman who has just walked into their house is nuts.

'Of course we knew you were coming.'

'Okay, that's great, well, this is Simon - he is one of the other guys who was at the funeral, and this is my best friend Juan. My boyfriend, Ted, is waiting outside.'

'Oh. You brought your boyfriend and your friends? Right. Okay. I don't really know what funeral you're talking about, and where's all your stuff?'

'In the hotel,' I reply.

'You'll need it, won't you?'

'Will I?'

'To do my hair. Isn't that why you're here?'

'You want me to do your hair?' I reply. It's all a bit surreal, but if she wants me to do her hair, I'll give it a go.

As we're miscommunicating, a lady in overalls, clutching a large toolbox comes piling through the door, apologising for being late in such a strong Welsh accent that I can't work out whether it's real, or whether she's putting it on for comedy effect. She looks around the room before focusing on dark stripe lady.

'You must be Bronwyn? I'm Melissa...from Melissa's Manes on the High Street. I've come to do your roots.'

'Oh,' exclaims the woman with the dark stripe who we now know to be called Bronwyn. She has a look of confusion on her heavily painted face as she turns to me. 'So, if this is Melissa - who the hell are you? I thought you were the hairdresser.'

'Do you mind if I sit down? Then I can explain.'

Bronwyn looks doubtful...which is fair enough. Why should she allow a total stranger to sit down in her house?

'I'll be really quick,' I offer. 'My name's Mary and I was invited to a stranger's funeral around a year ago...'

'You probably don't need to go into all that,' whispers Simon.

'Okay then. Well, to keep it short - we are looking for the Gower family. They used to live here and we wondered whether you had any idea where they'd moved to after leaving here.'

'We've no idea,' says the other girl. 'Some private detectives came here looking for them around a year ago. I explained to them that we are renting the house from Sam Taylor, who lives over by there; over the road. We don't know anyone who lived here before.'

'Did the detectives talk to Sam Taylor?' I ask.

'I think so, but Sam has only had the house for a couple of years and he'd never heard of the Gower family either, so they left. Are you detectives? Are the Gower family criminals or something?'

'Gosh - no, not criminals. We're trying to find them because they are owed money.'

'Right,' says Bronwyn. 'This all sounds well dodgy to me.'

· · ·

Despite Simon's earlier insistence that it was not necessary, I decide that it is, and start to regale Melissa with the story of the Gower family, the mysterious invitation, the funeral, the money, and how incredibly kind the Gower family had been to Reginald's parents.

Melissa works on Bronwyn's highlights, while the two of them listen to me, entranced.

'The dead guy sounds like a blinking lunatic, but I love the story of his dad coming over here and everything.'

'I know, right?'

'It's so odd that no one has been able to find the Gower family. Where do you think they are?'

'I've really no idea. We thought we'd come here today just to see whether we could find them. I don't know whether you know anyone who's lived in the area for a long time who could help us at all?'

'Of course. This is so exciting. I feel like Inspector Poirot. Let me ring Grandma, she knows people who have lived in the area for years.'

'Thank you so much.'

I call Ted in from outside where he has been languishing against a lamp post, and he joins Simon and I on the sofa, while Juan perches on a small stool with his legs all wrapped around each other as if he'd knotted them. We sit there, in a stranger's house, waiting patiently, while the scent of bleach fills the air.

Bronwyn talks in Welsh on the phone while the three of us listen in silence, trying to detect any words that might allow us to understand how the conversation is going.

'When did you say they lived here?' asks Bronwyn.

'We know they moved here soon after the war, so late 40s,

early-50s. Unfortunately we don't know how long they stayed here.'

Bronwyn returns to the call and chats away while Simon, Ted and I sit, poised on the edges of our seats. Juan is no longer seated. He has jumped up and is assisting in the hair regrowth touch up, by passing the foils to the hairdresser. Finally the call ends.

'Okay,' she says. 'It's looking good. My Nan's got a fancy man called John Morgan who is in a nursing home, and he used to live round here just after the war so might remember them arriving. Visiting time at the home is at 2pm. My Nan told me to tell you that John's memory is not the best, but it's worth a try. Okay?'

'Yes, yes. That would be great,' I say. 'Thank you. Have you got the address?'

'Here you go,' says Bronwyn, scribbling it down on a piece of paper. 'We'll see you there at 2pm. You won't recognise me, mind. My hair will be lovely.'

'Thank you,' I say, clutching the piece of paper and preparing to leave.

'Let me just finish these foils,' says Juan. 'I'll be five minutes.'

Ted, Simon and I stand there while Juan plays Vidal Sassoon.

'You've been very helpful,' Melissa tells him. 'Can I ask you something?'

'Of course you can, my love.'

'I'd like to whisper it, please.'

Juan moves in and listens attentively, nodding as Melissa talks, before hugging her affectionately.

'Of course you can, honey,' he says, handing her a foil, and moving over to collect some more.

'She asked whether she could come to the nursing home with us this afternoon. I told her that's fine.'

'Of course,' I say, concerned that we will be going fairly mob-handed to this nursing home this afternoon, and that might not be the wisest move considering the age of the guy we're going to see.

'Now are you okay to do the rest of these foils without me? We'll see you at the nursing home at 2pm.'

# CHAPTER 7

# $\mathcal{M}$eeting John Morgan: Present Day

At 2pm we're standing outside *Gwerin Gyfeillgar Nursing Home* on the outskirts of Llandrindod Wells. Have you ever heard of a more Welsh-sounding place? We manage to get lost finding it, of course, so have to keep asking people if they know where it is. Ted and I put Juan in charge of all direction-related enquiries, just for the sheer joy of hearing our lovely Spanish dancer friend try to get his mouth around the Welsh pronunciations with a lilting Mediterranean accent. None of the people he asks understand a word that he is saying. The whole thing is a joy to watch. While Juan grapples with the native tongue, Simon drives us (very slowly, while wearing his driving gloves) in a Vauxhall Astra built for people half our sizes.

I think both Simon and his car are pleased when we make it.

I notice him wincing at the groan emanating from the suspension when Ted and I get in. I'm not sure his little car has ever experienced anything quite like it before.

The girls are waiting for us in Melissa's adorable pink van with 'Melissa's Manes' written in italic on the side, along with various pictures of hairdressing paraphernalia scribed in gold ink: there's a hair dryer, a lady in rollers, brushes and combs - all in glittery gold.

'Isn't it magnificent?' says Bronwyn, gently stroking the outside of Melissa's van. 'I've never seen anything so lovely before. Have you?'

Bronwyn looks much better with her hair done. It's a lovely honey-blonde colour and all swishy and healthy-looking. It's a shame she's done her makeup in such an odd way, with thick black eyeliner extending over her eyes and flicking up towards her eyebrows and a really dark lipstick that completely washes her out.

'Right, let's go. I should warn you that John Morgan likes to be called John Morgan, never John, for some reason. He's very old, so you have to talk in a loud voice, and use simple language or he won't know what's going on and he'll start talking about the war, or something.'

'Sure,' I say. 'I love old people. I met this guy called Frank on a cruise once - he was nearly ninety, and he was great. I spent the whole cruise with him.'

We walk through the corridors, taking in the smells of cabbage and antiseptic that grace the air in all old people's homes. We come to flat seven and knock gently on the door. A carer greets us, carrying a tray of crockery.

'Oh goodness, John Morgan, you've got lots of lovely ladies to see you,' she says to him.

Ted coughs lightly.

'Sorry, lots of ladies and one man,' she corrects herself. Juan shrugs, and pulls his floppy felt hat down further over his ears.

Mr. Morgan is very old. I know that is stating the obvious. But he really is quite the oldest person I've ever seen. His eyes are like those of a child, peering out from bunched up, and wrinkled skin. He looks sort of like an iguana, but I keep this observation to myself. He sits in front of us, without moving or commenting.

'Thank you for letting us come to see you,' I say, leaning over and putting my hand out. His hands stay firmly in his lap so I just smile. 'My name is Mary.'

'I know that,' he said in a lovely baritone voice, the depth of which belies its owner's fading health. 'You want to know all about the Gower family?'

'Yes, do you know them? Gosh, I wasn't sure whether you'd have come across them.'

'Yes – farmers, weren't they? Came over from Gower after the war. I remember the lady very well. She was an attractive one. Always in her smart clothes. All the boys fancied her but I never quite trusted her. There was something about her that wasn't quite right. They had a young son.'

'Yes, that's right. The son and the father were called Tom. Apparently they called the son Tom Junior.'

'They called him TJ. But I didn't. I called him Tom Junior.'

'You don't know what became of them, do you?'

'Yes, I remember very clearly. They upped and moved down to the south coast, because he had a job at Portsmouth University. We were all very impressed - a university. Teaching farming or something, he was. And that Tom Junior, he had a job working somewhere too. I can't remember where, but it was definitely Portsmouth they went to. Not that long ago, actually.'

'Really? They've only just left here, have they?'

'Yes - very recent. Must have been in the early 60s, I'd guess.'

'The early 60s?' we chorus. To us that feels like a million years ago, where to him it clearly seems like yesterday.

I try to ask John Morgan about Irene and why he didn't trust her; more out of nosiness than anything else. But all he'll say is that he liked Tom a lot, and he liked to talk about farming with him, whenever he got the chance. 'Tom loved to chat about the farm he had in Gower. I know he wished they'd never left. He shouldn't have. He shouldn't have listened to Irene, he should have stood his ground. But, my-oh-my, you should have seen her. I guess she was difficult to turn down, with her miniskirts and boots and her fancy hair and what not.'

He spoke about Irene until his eyes began to close and his shoulders drooped in weariness. He yawned gently and I could see he was starting to nod off.

'You'll need to leave now,' said the nurse. 'He's exhausted.'

'Of course,' I say. We all bid him a fond farewell, blow kisses and wave, but he's gone, drifted off into sleep.

'I've brought these chocolates for him,' I say, handing the nurse a giant box of Maltesers. 'My friend Frank used to love Maltesers. I thought John might. Frank said he loved them because he could suck them if he didn't have his teeth in, and they tasted just as good.  If he doesn't like them, please keep them yourself. You've been very kind to help us like this.'

'Oh, thank you,' she says. 'I hope you find your friends.'

We trundle out of the nursing home, welcoming the cool air as we step onto the pavement. The place is heated to boiling point.

'Come on,' says Simon, leading us all away from the building and to the bench in a small meditation garden they have set up, presumably for springtime when the flowers are out and the sun is shining, and relatives bring their elderly relatives out to get some fresh air. This time of year it is all empty.

We sit down and look at one another.

'Okay, well at least we know where the family went,' I say.

'Yes, we know where he went in 1960. We don't know where he is now.'

'No, I know that, but we've got significantly more to work on now than we had when we first came. We could contact Portsmouth University and see whether they have contact details for someone who worked at the college in the early 60s? I know it all sounds a bit unlikely, but you never know.

'This morning we didn't know we were going to walk into a nursing home and talk to someone who knows the Gower family. We've done better than the private detectives already. We should be pleased.'

'You're absolutely right,' says Ted, protectively. 'You should all be very pleased with what you've found out, and now we know they're not here, we can stop looking for them and start enjoying ourselves. I'm up for a boozy, late lunch if anyone else is?'

'Oh, I definitely am,' says Juan. 'More booze than lunch if you don't mind.'

'Me too,' says Melissa, in a move which surprises all of us.

'Me three,' says Bronwyn.

'Sure, yes, lunch sounds great, but I was thinking that we could make some enquiries about the Gower family first? I mean, I was even thinking that if the family is still based down there, we could head for the south coast tomorrow.'

'You really think we should do that?' says Simon, somewhat agitated by the proposal.

'Well, depending on what we find out - yes. Simon – it's just you and me, Ted, Juan. We are treating this like a mini holiday so it's no problem for us to go down to the south coast. If you're up for it, I think we should go.'

'This has got the feeling of a wild goose chase about it,' says Ted. 'We can't keep chasing from one place to the next.'

'I'm not saying that. All I'm suggesting is that we make a few calls.'

'Come on then. Shall we head back to the hotel?'

'Sure,' I say.

'Yep, okay. We'll follow you,' says Melissa.

I climb into Simon's car and wait patiently while he puts on his gloves and adjusts his mirror. There is something quite soothing about his attention to detail. It reminds me of sitting in my grandparents' car when I was younger, waiting as they made every adjustment, checked the petrol and water and treated every short journey as if they were about to embark on a trek through Africa.

Back at the hotel, we gather in reception to discuss the options. The group is of three minds at this point...there's me who thinks we should hot-foot it to Southsea and keep hot-footing it in pursuit of the Gower family, then there's Juan, Ted and Simon who think we should stay exactly where we are and have a nice relaxing time. Finally there's Bronwyn and Melissa who are just glad to be at the party.

Back at the hotel, we order coffees and teas in reception, and set about making a plan. I call Portsmouth University and ask to be put through to the Department of Agriculture and Farming. There is a lengthy pause.

'We don't have a department like that. The closest thing would be land management. Shall I put you through to them?'

'Sure,' I reply.

I go through to land management where a woman who sounds exactly the same as the last person, tells me that the University no longer runs agricultural courses, they are all run by Portsmouth Agricultural College.

'But I'm sure he worked at the university.'

'Well, I'd need to know what department, and there isn't an agricultural and farming department - that's all done at the college.'

I explain briefly that we were trying to locate someone who worked there at the beginning of the 1960s.

'The agricultural college will have all the records relating to that time,' she says.

I thank her for her time and turn to the posse. 'Okay, we need to call another number. It's a separate agricultural college.'

I go through the same routine again, asking whether there is anyone there who might be able to confirm that a Tom Gower worked there. The woman clicks on a few keys, I hear voices, then more key clicking. 'Yes, he did.'

Found him, I whisper to the group

'Would you have any idea where he went when he left? Is he still in touch with the college? Do you know whether he still lives locally?'

'I don't know any of those things, to be honest,' she says. 'Why are you so keen to reach him? Did he teach you?'

'Yes, that's right.'

'Well you're welcome to come down and look through the paperwork here. It's all on microfiche, I'm afraid, but there are records going back to the 50s, so it might help you.'

'Great,' I say, giving the others a thumbs up. 'I look forward to seeing you soon.'

I end the call and look at the group. 'I really, really think we should go to Southsea. They knew all about him and said there was a lot of information there.'

Okay, okay, so that was a bit of a lie, but I knew I had to say something to motivate them, and persuade them to make the journey. Simon responds by sighing deeply.

'If we do decide to go, we will never all get in my car,' he says. 'I'm not sure I'd trust that thing to go all the way to the south coast with just me in it, let alone you three as well...' I swear he glances at my stomach when he says that.

'We could come with you,' says Melissa. 'I'm not working for the next few days, and I've got a van, in which we do beauty treatments and hair care on the road, so it's got seats, and there's lots of room in it. And I've never been to England.'

'We saw your van at the old people's home. That sounds perfect,' I say, while Simon and Ted exchange glances.

'Are you sure you don't mind driving? It's a long way.'

'Is it? Is it further than Cardiff?'

'It's a hell of a lot further than Cardiff. It's on the south coast of England. I'm not sure this is such a good idea,' says Simon.

'Well I can start driving, and if I get fed up someone else can drive. The van is insured regular as we all share it.'

'By 'regular' you mean that anyone is insured to drive? We should definitely check that.'

'Aye, it'll be fine, but we'll go and check.'

The two girls leave and we all look at one another. 'Is anyone else surprised by the fact that a random hairdresser is offering to drive us to Portsmouth in her pink van?' says Simon. 'I don't mean to be ungrateful, but it seems most peculiar.'

BERNICE BLOOM

'Yes, I don't think we should take her up on it,' says Ted. 'We don't know what we're going to find when we get to Portsmouth, it might be a wasted trip. It seems very odd to have Melissa and Bronwyn with us.'

'But they want to come,' I say. I like the idea of them coming along. I'd have female company, we'd be able to get down there in the van, and also because I am hoping that Melissa might give me some of those gorgeous blonde highlights that transformed Bronwyn's hair.

'They're the people who live in the Gower's house now, and they introduced us to John Morgan, so I can see why they're interested.'

'Yes, I suppose,' says Simon. 'But I still think it will be a waste of time.'

'Yes, I vote very strongly that we don't go,' says Ted.

'I vote that we do.'

# CHAPTER 8

ff to Southsea: Present Day

It's quite a perilous journey to Southsea from mid-Wales. Well, it certainly is when the woman driving you has never previously driven more than about 20 miles and has neither understanding of, nor respect for, the speedometer. The van shakes and rattles as she practically stands on the accelerator pedal, flying through rural streets en route to the motorway. 'I've never driven on a motorway before,' Melissa says with glee as she jumps the car onto a busy roundabout, inches ahead of a Tesco's van.

Then she drives onto the M4 and it turns out she quite likes it. We know this from the wild squeal she emits as she moves into the second lane, overtaking the traffic in the inside lane and waving madly at them with her beautifully manicured hands.

Even Bronwyn is looking scared at this point. Up until now, she's been enjoying the thrill of the pedal to floor experience, but she's looking deeply uncomfortable now.

'Darling, you don't have to wave every time you overtake someone,' says Juan. 'Your arm will become incredibly tired if you do that every time you overtake.'

'I know, but it's so flipping great going past these big lorries. I can't help it.'

'So, you really haven't driven on the motorway before? This is your first time?'

'Yes, I just drive around the town, going to different people's houses to do their hair and beauty. I've never needed to go on the motorway, and I didn't pass my test that long ago.'

'When did you pass it?'

'Last Wednesday,' she says, still waving like the Queen as she overtakes a car with a large caravan on the back.

'Right, well, you need to tell us when you get tired, and someone else will drive for you. It would be unwise for you to drive for too long if you haven't been driving for that long.'

'Oh, I've been driving for a long time, I just didn't pass my test til recently.'

'You were driving around before passing your test?'

'Yes,' she says calmly, as she negotiates a lane change with little regard for the other traffic on the motorway.

'You know, Melissa, maybe I should drive for a little while, we don't want you to get too tired,' Ted says.

Melissa says, 'Okeydokey,' and pulls into the inside lane, moving to within inches of the bonnet of the car she has just overtaken, forcing them to beep and grind to a halt. She pulls onto the hard shoulder and comes to an emergency stop, throwing us all forward in our seats.

Melissa swings open the driver's door while Ted shouts, 'No, you can't do that...' But it's too late, Melissa's door is wide open and she is out and running around to jump in the back of the van with the rest of us. Cars on the motorway are forced to swerve around the open door.

When the back doors of the van open, I jump out and get into the passenger seat, and Ted slides over to take the driving role. We pull back onto the motorway, and though it was incredibly kind of Melissa to drive us, and very generous of her to let us use her van, there isn't a person in that bubble-gum pink motor-vehicle who does not give an almighty sigh of relief as Ted moves seamlessly into the traffic, indicating and checking his mirror as he goes, then moving into the middle lane, without waving at any of the vehicles on the road. We soon pass the caravan-towing car that Melissa had almost written off five minutes earlier, and I see them glance over warily, but Ted continues, building up speed until we are moving at the same speed as all the traffic on the road and are far less of a hazard.

In the end, Ted does all the driving. The plan was for him to swap with Simon at the service station. But Simon spends most of the journey complaining how fast Ted is going every time he nudges close to 70, so we are all very pleased when Ted offers to do the rest of the driving. I think Simon is too, for all his moaning about the speed, he doesn't seem all that keen to take the reins. I witnessed Simon's driving yesterday. If he'd been behind the steering wheel we'd have taken most of the week to reach the south coast. As it happens, we climb, weary and with aching limbs from the back of the pink van at around 6pm.

We've been driving all day, but at least we had a decent break for lunch, and are in Southsea in time for dinner. And yes – you are right – I do measure all journeys by the distance they are between meals!

We park the van along the seafront, outside the Sunnyside Hotel, the cheapest one we could find. I'm not sure why we were desperate to find a cheap hotel, since we inherited hundreds of thousands of pounds a year ago, but Simon is one of those guys who could inherit 40 million and still wear the shoes he had worn since he was 14. I didn't want to rock the boat by suggesting that we could all step up a notch and get a nice place.

The good news is that Simon and I have decided that we will cover the cost of the girls' hotel and food, because they've been kind enough to come with us. They have been so helpful so far. And they're an entertaining duo. And they have a van. And Melissa does such good highlights.

Ted removes the bags from the back of the van and starts to carry them all to the hotel. 'There's no need to carry everyone's bags,' I say, taking mine out of his hands.

'No, we can manage,' say the girls, stepping forward to take theirs, while Simon walks on, into the reception. Ted walks behind him carrying his bag. I look at the girls and we stifle a laugh. Simon is the most extraordinary guy, completely self-unaware, kind and lovely, but daft as a brush.

Ted phrases it differently: 'All the girls are managing to carry their bags, and I'm carrying a bloke's. What's wrong with him?'

The hotel is like something out of the 1950s, so we opt out of staying there for dinner, and find a nice little café on the seafront instead. It is called Shambles and proudly boasts that it has been there, in the same spot, since 1962.

'Tom and Irene might have come in here,' I comment.

'They could be here tonight,' says Simon, and a sudden knot forms in my stomach. It's like that feeling you get when you're out somewhere and you're told a boy you fancy might be coming. You know - that ball you get inside you that's a mixture of fear and excitement. Well that's how I feel right now. I really want us to find the Gower family.

'It would be so amazing. Just - so incredible,' I say, while scanning the restaurant for a young man in farming dungarees and wellington boots.

'You know that the chances of Tom or Irene being alive are very remote, don't you?' says Simon. 'We're tracing where they lived in order to find their descendants.'

'Yes, but I don't really want to think about that. I want to think about actually seeing them.'

Ted leans over and squeezes my shoulder.

We are sitting at a far table, against the floor to ceiling windows which give us an excellent view of the beach. We watch as waves slap up toward the windows as we sit there enjoying lovely wine and nice food. We're all out tonight except for Juan, who wants to do an online yoga and meditation class instead.

As the others chat and laugh, I sit back and retreat into a dream world...back in the 1960s with Irene sunbathing on the beach and Tom Junior swimming in the sea. It must have been a lovely place to grow up.

'We have to find them. I can sense that they are here some-where,' I say. 'Wouldn't it be brilliant? I feel so excited I could scream.'

'Let's not start screaming yet, let's look at the information we've got so far.' says Simon. 'What do we know, and what do we need to find out?'

'I think we need to head down to Portsmouth Agricultural College first thing in the morning,' I say. 'That'll give us a better idea of things, and hopefully we'll find someone who knew him, or Irene.'

'Sure,' says Simon. 'Let's start there. We could also check births, marriages and deaths in case there's anything listed in that time.'

'They can't be dead,' I say, rather louder than I mean to, but I do feel strongly about finding them.

'I know how keen you are to find them, angel,' says Ted, stroking my arm. As I lean over to give him a kiss on the cheek, both Simon's phone and my phone bleep in unison on the table in front of us, indicating that there is a message in the 'mysterious invitation' group.

There's a message from Sally Bramley.

'I've decided to come and join you. Which hotel in Llandrindod are you staying at?'

I look at Simon. He is still struggling to remember his code to get his phone open so I explain the nature of the message that has been left.

'Shall I go back to her and explain?' I say.

'Yes please,' he says, removing his reading glasses and laying his phone back down on the table, relieved that he doesn't have to tangle with new technology.


*Mysterious Invitation WhatsApp Group*

. . .

**Mary Brown**

Hi everyone, just a quick update for anyone thinking of coming to join us. We're in Southsea. I know, I know! We only stayed in Llandrindod for one night before discovering that the Gower family moved from their home there in the 1960s. They moved to Southsea which is on the south coast, near Portsmouth. So that's where we are. Come and join us, Sally. We're at the Sunnyside Hotel.

From the Southsea Six! :)


**Sally Bramley**

Oh wow. That's much easier. Yes, I'll definitely come and join you. I'll be there around 10am tomorrow. Shall I just come straight to the hotel?


**Mary Brown**

Yes, we'll be in the breakfast room. Come and join us for coffee. Can't wait to see you. X


**Sally Bramley**

PS Who are the six? I'm confused! Is everyone there but me? In that case, are there not five of you? X


**Mary Brown**

Oh, sorry - no. There's me and Simon, then my boyfriend Ted is here and my lovely friend Juan. Also, there's a woman called Bronwyn who was living in the Gower's old house in

Llandrindod, who knew someone who said the Gower family had moved to Southsea, and her hairdresser called Melissa who drove us all down here in her van.

**Sally Bramley**

Wow. That sounds like a riot.

# CHAPTER 9

 ig Decisions: 1970

'Hello, Grants Estate Agents. Irene Gower speaking, can I help you?'

There was a pause while Irene nodded, listening as the house-seller detailed his concerns.

'Sure, I understand, Mr. Davis...' she replied, as she heard how he didn't want to drop the asking price, but he was worried about the fact that so few people had been round to view his property.

Irritation had crept into his voice, as if the lack of interest in his house was entirely her doing. As if she were not sending people round on purpose.

'We're doing all we can,' she said. The trouble was that Mr. Davis's house was a poorly-decorated, old-fashioned bungalow, and though it was in a decent location, and was roomy inside, the decor was pre-war and very unappealing. It reminded her of going to Tom's house, when they were first courting. The farm house had been a whirl of yellow floral wallpaper that had made her wince when she walked inside.

Mr. Davis's place was worse: in the bedroom there was blue wallpaper on the walls that extended right across the ceiling, and the curtains matched: they were exactly the same sky blue colour and with an identical floral pattern. It looked more like a dolls house than a home for a modern family.

In its day, it had probably been all the rage - that twee early 50s look of endless floral and chintzy wallpaper had been everywhere. But this was the 70s now, and the more discerning clientele were opting for much trendier interiors.

'Do you remember we mentioned that it might be nice to decorate?' Irene asked, cautiously. 'Sort of spruce the place up a bit and make it look more modern?'

'What a waste of money,' said Mr. Davis. 'The place is neat and tidy and it's always clean. If someone who moves in here wants to decorate, that's their prerogative, but I'm certainly not going to do it when I'm about to move out. Where's the sense in that? Can you put me through to your boss? I'm not prepared to talk to his secretary anymore.'

Irene signalled to Mark that she was putting a call through to him. She wasn't Mark's secretary, and the horrible Mr. Davis was well aware of that. She wasn't going to fight against his misogynistic words though, she'd done enough of that in the years that she'd worked here. Now she'd given in her notice and had just a month left, she'd spend those weeks rising above the aggro and sexism that had defined her time working at Mark's estate agency, smile and move on.

She looked over at Mark, still deep in conversation with Mr. Davis, and tapped her watch to indicate that she was leaving. He nodded that it was fine, then gave her a thumbs up, just to be really clear. He was such an incredibly lovely man. She knew he was heartbroken that she had decided to leave the firm. She'd been honest with him, and told him that she had decided to try to make her marriage work, and that they might move away. He'd looked devastated, but he had never held it against her. He hadn't asked for any details. He'd just said that he understood.

Irene grabbed her mac and her handbag and left the office.

Outside it was colder than she had expected, so she slipped on her mac and looked away as a car sped past full of rowdy young men beeping their horn and shouted as they raced past.

She was wearing her new white patent leather boots, the ones that Mark had bought her, with lovely big buttons on the side. They went so well with her black mac with white piping. She loved looking fashionable, but could do without the jeers and lame comments from passing men.

Irene walked along the seafront, past the bench that she and Mark now called 'our bench', pausing to think of everything that had happened since she met Mark here. Life was so complicated. But Mark was a good person. She would never regret meeting him or spending time getting to know him.

She glanced at her watch. The appointment was in five minutes, so she kept walking, into the centre of Southsea, along Palace Road and through the familiar yellow door, up the rickety stairs and into the waiting room. Tom was already there. His face lit up when he saw her.

'You look lovely,' he mouthed, so as not to be heard by the

others, waiting, like him, for an appointment with the marriage guidance counsellor.

She smiled as she sat down, slipping her sunglasses off her nose and up into her long brown hair, and reaching for a magazine.

'Tom and Irene Gower, please.'

There was a sigh from a young man in the room who clearly thought it was his turn. Irene lay down the magazine, stood up and followed her husband into the room.

'How are you feeling?' asked Dr Kent, the marriage guidance counsellor who had been advising them for the past few months, as they struggled to get their marriage back on track.

'I feel okay,' said Irene.

'Have you moved back into the family home yet?'

'No,' said Irene. 'But I have given in my notice at work. Just a few more weeks to go.'

'That's a very positive step. How is that making you feel?'

'I feel a bit nervous about everything at the moment. I have been working at the estate agency for quite a few years, and Mark has been a good friend to me.'

Tom grunted.

'It's true, Tom. We've been over this many times. Nothing has ever happened between us. He's a friend, and he's my boss. I moved out of the house because we were arguing all the time, not because of Mark. I needed to get my head together. It was never because of Mark.'

Irene was aware of how angry Tom was about her friendship with Mark. TJ had seen them swimming in the sea one time and taken it badly, assumed she was having an affair and told Tom. There appeared to be nothing she could do to convince him that there was no affair. Mark was a friend, and that was all.

'Is there anything else bothering you?' asked the doctor. 'You said that everything is making you feel nervous at the moment.'

'Just the usual worries. My son TJ is living in Brighton with his wife, Yvonne, and I miss them. He doesn't call much. He blames me for everything that happened, of course. They've got a little boy called Andrew who is 18 months old, and his wife is heavily pregnant with their next one. I wish I could be more involved...'

'How does it make you feel when you're not very involved?'

'I feel shut out, I feel like I've lost my son and lost my husband and wrecked my family, but I didn't do anything wrong.'

'You had an affair.' said Tom. He said this every time. Every time.

Irene felt her sadness turn to anger. 'No I didn't. I met a friend, and the friend offered me a job. That's all.'

'But he wanted to have an affair with you. You can't pretend he didn't.'

'Tom, we've been over this and over it. I didn't have an affair with anyone. He might have wanted to, but I didn't. Never. I wasn't even tempted. I was flattered by his attention at the beginning, but we fell into a friendship very quickly.'

'And have you made a decision about Brighton yet?'

Irene looked down at her hands at this question, so the counsellor looked instead at Tom.

'I've been offered early retirement from Portsmouth College, and some part time work at a college in Brighton, if I want it,' he said. 'And the Brighton Argus want me to do some cartoons for them. We'll have enough money. Yvonne won't have to work. The kids are settled there and our grandchildren are there. We should go.'

'How about you, Irene?'

Irene continued to stare down at her hands. 'It feels risky.'

'Risky in what way?'

'Well - we'll move to a place where we don't know many people, and will be stuck together, and it might be the end of it all.'

'It might not,' said Tom. 'It could be the making of us...'

Irene looked over at him. She'd made her mind up about moving along the coast, but she didn't want to discuss it now. She planned to talk to Tom directly, not through their counsellor.

But Tom seemed so small and helpless, slumped in the chair, practically begging her to do something to help save their marriage, and she didn't want to wait any longer.

'I've given in my notice at the estate agents. I think we should move to Brighton.'

Tom's grey eyes widened and a smile spread across the entire width of his face. She might never be in love with this man again, she might not feel a rush of excitement when he walked into the room, but he was her husband, and this was her family. And this was her chance to put everything right.

'Let's move to Brighton,' she confirmed.

The counsellor asked her why, of course. All the counsellor seemed to do was ask why she was doing things and how it all made her feel.

'Because I think it would do us all a lot of good. It would enable me to spend more time with TJ and Yvonne, and give us a very real chance of repairing our relationship.'

'And how do you feel when you say that?' asked the counsellor.

'I feel good,' she said, because saying anything else would have opened up the gates of interrogation even further. In truth, she felt nervous. She had moved out of the family home a few years ago when TJ moved to Brighton because it had become unbearable. Tom would accuse her of cheating on a daily basis because she worked with Mark every day, and Tom knew they went swimming together in the mornings. In truth, nothing had happened between her and Mark.

Not once.

The only thing she'd lied to Tom about was telling him that she'd never fancied Mark, and never wanted anything to happen. That was wholly untrue. She'd desperately wanted something to happen. Desperately. But she was always constrained by the vows she'd made all those years ago, and her sense of devotion and propriety.

'I wish you well,' said the counsellor. 'I'm always here if you need me, or I can refer you to someone in Brighton, if that would be easier.'

They walked single file down the old stairs and out to a bright and sunny day.

'I'll miss Southsea,' she said.

'But Brighton's beautiful,' replied Tom. 'Are you coming home, now?'

'I've got something to do first,' she said. 'I'll come over later.'

Irene walked over the phone box and rang Mark.

'Can you meet me at our bench?' she said. 'I have something to tell you.'

# CHAPTER 10

$\mathcal{L}$ife in Brighton: 1973

Irene walked back from the telephone box with her hands pushed deep into her pockets and her collar up despite the warmth of the midday sun: shielding herself from the world. It was as if she were hiding away; protecting a great, dark secret. She let herself into the roomy apartment that she and Tom were renting, and slumped across the sofa.

'Where've you been?' asked Tom.

'For a walk on the seafront,' she said. It wasn't a lie. She went on regular walks along the seafront, but they always ended with her in the phone box, ringing Mark. She never mentioned that bit. Or how much she missed him.

'Are you ready for this lunch?'

'I'll get ready now. I won't be long.'

Irene knew exactly what she would wear: she slipped on her new flared trousers, some wedge shoes and a fitted polo neck jumper in a lovely burnt orange colour. It wasn't what most people would be wearing, but she didn't care. She wanted to look fashionable. It's what Jane would have wanted. She threw a crocheted handbag over her shoulder and headed back into the sitting room.

Tom stood and looked her up and down.

'Is that appropriate?' he said.

'Why wouldn't it be?'

'I don't know. It's a memorial service for Jane. Won't people be dressed more formally? I'm wearing a jacket and tie. I got the impression that others would be, too.'

'You want me to wear a jacket and tie?'

'No, of course not. I'm sure you're fine dressed the way you are. You look very fashionable. Come on, let's go.'

Irene sighed heavily, as if to emphasise her frustration at him, while he led the way down the stairs and out of their pretty Brighton flat. But she knew deep down that he was right. She probably should have dressed more soberly, but she didn't want to sit and remember Jane while dressed in black. Jane was so vibrant, joyful and wonderful.

Irene had become very close to Yvonne's mother, Jane, since moving to Brighton. The two of them had become insepara-ble...meeting for drinks and in cafes for cups of tea, and dancing in clubs until the early hours of the morning.

But then, a year ago, Jane died. It was sudden and unex-pected - a stroke brought on by a blood disorder that no one knew she had. Something called Factor V Leiden, inherited from both her parents, it turned out, which made it particularly dangerous. In the year since Jane's death, the family had investigated the blood disorder and ruminated many times, over many drinks, on how, if only they had known, they could've done something about it.

They could have sought treatment, had her monitored regularly by her doctor, done anything within their power to stop her from dying such a sudden, brutal death at such a young age. But no one had known. How could they?

Simon, Yvonne's father, who Irene had also got on with well, had become withdrawn and quiet since his wife's death, no longer the active member of their family group, organising get-togethers, walks along the beach, barbecues and picnics. He was a lovely man, very kind and good fun, and Irene liked him enormously, but she hated the way he had become such a shadow of his former self since losing his wife. Today, there was a small gathering at Simon's to remember Jane, one year on.

'Sorry,' she said to Tom, as they sat in traffic just minutes from Simon's house. 'I should have dressed in black. You're right. It's just that I can't bear that she is gone. I can't bear the reality of her not being there with Simon anymore. She always wore such bright, modern and lovely clothes. I guess I wanted to reflect that. But you're right. You're absolutely right. I'm sorry I snapped at you.'

Tom smiled at her and squeezed her knee in an affectionate gesture. 'I know you were very close to her, and I understand. Don't worry, you'll be the best dressed person there as you always are, wherever we go.'

There were around 20 people gathered at Simon's house. All of them in black. Sod them. Irene was wearing the most modern outfit she owned because that's what Jane would have wanted. She wondered whether any of these people really knew Jane like she did.

She glanced around the room at the familiar faces, nodding and smiling in recognition, while inside she felt she might shrivel up and die with the pain of all this. A year had gone by since Jane's death now, but she felt no closer to coping with the loss of her great friend.

Jane had kept her from crumbling when Irene had first moved to Brighton. Jane had been a joyful reminder that life could be fun and enjoyable.

One by one, Jane's closest friends walked to the front of the room and told stories about her, and the fun times they'd had. Irene told them about the time the two of them had gone out late, and begged the barman not to chuck them out at 10.30pm, urging him to give them one more drink until a loud voice behind them told them to go. They spun round to see a cross-looking policeman standing, glaring at them.

'Jane gave him a kiss on the cheek and we both ran out. He looked furious, but we ended up becoming really good friends with him.'

'You sure did!' came a loud voice. It was George - the officer they'd met that night.

Simon smiled, enjoying the memory of his lovely, sociable wife. He'd heard the stories of Jane and Irene's nights out before, and always enjoyed them. He loved the memories of his wife as this wonderful life force, this bringer-together of people. This kind, beautiful, gentle woman.

He looked over and caught Irene's eye, smiling warmly at her. He was so glad the two of them had come to mean so much to each other. He was aware how much colour, life and joy Irene had brought to Jane.

Irene returned the smile. She couldn't tell all of the stories to the assembled guests, not that they did anything terrible, but they hadn't always been the best behaved of people. For example, she couldn't talk about the time they drove to Southsea so that she could see Mark one last time. She could never tell them how Jane urged her to spend time alone with him while Jane went for a long walk along the seafront to give them space. She would never tell anyone what had happened. None of that would ever be shared with anyone.

# CHAPTER 11

emembering Jane: 1973


Irene had been so low when she first arrived in Brighton. No one knew how much she'd loved Mark. Then she told Jane, and they spoke about it endlessly. Jane never judged or commented, she just listened, and took Irene on nights out that allowed her to forget about everything and enjoy herself.

'Irene, is there anything else you'd like to say about Jane?'

Simon looked almost pleading as he spoke, as if desperate for Irene to continue with the tributes to his late wife.

'Of course,' she said, stepping forward to the front of the group. There was no story that she particularly wanted to tell, but for Simon's sake, she wanted to offer some words about the beautiful woman he'd lost.

'I didn't know Jane when I first moved to Brighton. Well, we knew each other through the kids, and obviously saw one another when the wedding was being planned, but we weren't close. We were very much parents of the marrying couple rather than friends.'

Irene paused to gather herself. She didn't want to cry. This wasn't a time for shedding tears, it was a time for recalling the beauty, joy and wonder of Jane.

'Then I moved to this town from a place where I'd had a job and lots of friends, and felt quite lonely. Jane picked me up and took me out and introduced me to everyone she knew.

'Gosh, in many ways it seems like an eternity since she died, and in other ways it feels like it was just last week. Life has changed so much without her here. I miss hearing her voice, seeing her, spending time with her, I miss just knowing that she exists in the world.

'People say that time is a great healer. Who are the people who say that? They are frauds. Time hasn't healed anything. The more time goes by, the more I miss her. I hate that her family will be growing without her to see, and every time anything happens to me, I long to share it with her and feel desperately sad that I can't.

The Jane-shaped hole in my life is still there - like a deep, raw, ugly wound that will never heal. All I'm able to do now is cope with the wound. I've learned not to prod it or to think about it all the time, and though it's always there and always will be, I can exist with it.

'I know that all of you will feel the same, because we all loved Jane deeply. You'll understand what I mean when I say that one of the hardest things is that people expect that you'll 'get over' it. The world moves on and slowly forgets the person you've loved so dearly and lost, but you never do. You remember. I remember. I always will.

'Not a day goes by that I don't think of her. Not a day goes by that I don't miss her. Not one single day. There will always be a void.'

There was loud applause when Irene finished her little speech but as she walked back to stand next to Tom, she felt disappointed. She hadn't meant to give a talk full of misery and woe. She'd meant to talk about the fun and joy of the woman.

'That was lovely,' said Tom.

'It was nowhere near lovely enough, it was all wrong,' she said. Then she watched as Tom's face fell. And realised she'd said the wrong thing again. The man must feel as if he could do nothing right at the moment.

'I just mean that I should have been a bit more upbeat,' said Irene. 'But - thanks.'

Irene looked up to see Yvonne waddling across the sitting room toward them. Her heavily pregnant tummy stood proud in front of her. This was to be her son's second child - a little girl.

'How's it going?' Irene asked

'As well as can be expected considering how rotten the whole damn thing is,' said Yvonne. 'Your words were lovely, thank you, Irene.'

'Gosh, it's the least I could do. I loved your mum very much.'

A silence settled between the women. Irene had always liked Yvonne, but she wasn't the easiest person to chat to. She seemed outgoing and lively when she first started dating TJ, but in company she was quite shy and never really spoke unless spoken to.

'How's the pregnancy going?' asked Irene.

BERNICE BLOOM

'Seven weeks to go. I'm just hoping and praying that she hasn't got the horrible blood thing that killed Mum.'

Blood tests, since Jane's death, had revealed that Yvonne had the disorder, but only mildly. Luckily their son, Andrew, didn't have it.

'Whatever happens, this little girl will be loved and cherished, and if she has the blood disorder, which seems really unlikely, then we'll deal with it, and get her the best treatment possible.'

Irene was cleaning the house, organising bags of old clothes to take to the charity shop, and throwing out anything that didn't have an immediate use, one bright morning in early May. She'd become a grandmother two weeks earlier to a lovely little girl called Sophia Jane. The baby had been born a few weeks earlier, but was putting on weight, and getting healthier every day.

Irene filled up another bag. It was such a small flat, she had to make sure there was no clutter lying around or it started to feel uncomfortably full. Then the phone rang.

'Hi, it's Simon,' said a small, shaky voice. 'We've had some bad news.'

'Oh no, what's happened?' said Irene, dropping the rubbish bag she held in her left hand and cupping the phone.

'It's the baby. Sophia Jane has the same blood disorder. She's got it badly. It's terrible news. I don't know what we're going to do.'

Irene listened as Simon explained the condition in detail. Sophia's disorder meant she was 20 times more likely to have a heart attack or stroke than if she had been born without the gene.

# CHAPTER 12

## New York calling: 1974

The months passed so quickly after the initial diagnosis. Spring
rolled into summer, before winter's frosty hands touched their
lives, then spring swept in again - majestically painting all the
colours back into their garden, into the sky and onto trees. It
was soon Sophia Jane's first birthday, and the third anniversary
of Jane's death, but the fact that the little girl's birthday fell so
close to the anniversary of her grandmother's death, meant that
thoughts of Jane were warmer and less fraught this time. Irene
still sobbed, alone, as she thought of her friend, but it was hard
to be morbid when pink balloons and teddy bears filled her son
and daughter-in-law's house.

'Come for dinner next week,' said Yvonne. 'It would be

lovely to see you and Tom when the kids are in bed and we can talk properly.'

'Of course. What a lovely idea. Will Simon be there?'

'Yes, I'll make sure he's there, too.'

Tom smiled warmly when she told him about the dinner. He was in such a good mood all the time these days. He'd been working more and more for the Brighton Argus, producing cartoons for them every day. They had even given him the title of 'Art Director (cartoons)' and Tom was to find good new cartoonists as well as producing his own pieces of art. Nothing fazed him. He was happy, content and loving life.

The day of the dinner, Irene sensed something was wrong. She tried to dismiss her negative feelings because she was well aware that she had a tendency to expect the worst. But when they arrived at her son's house, the feelings multiplied...there was a tension in the air and a feeling of doom all around.

TJ and Yvonne sat quietly, close together and holding hands, at dinner, something which Irene was quietly pleased about. She'd feared that their announcement would be that they were splitting up. She couldn't think of anything else quite dramatic enough to warrant this demand for an evening get-together.

'We've got some news,' said TJ suddenly, prompting all talking to stop, and all heads to swivel in his direction.

'We have been told that treatment for Sophia and Yvonne's illness is available.'

'Oh, that's amazing,' said Tom, jumping to his feet. 'I'm so pleased. What will it involve? When can she have it?'

'There's a small problem, and this is the bit you're not going to like. There is a treatment available but it's in America, at the Bellevue Hospital in New York,' said TJ.

Tom sat down while the others looked on in silence. 'We've

done lots of research and we've talked about it endlessly, and we think we should go.'

'But, how long would you be there for? What about work?' said Irene. She struggled to share Tom's instant delight in the idea. Of course, Sophia's health meant everything, but the family had established themselves so well in Brighton, they had so many friends and TJ was happy and successful. Was it worth them upping and moving to the other side of the world?

'Will it be expensive?' she asked.

'No,' said Yvonne, in her first foray into the conversation. 'I was talking to Dad about it and he thinks we might be able to go there without any charge, under the new healthcare policy in the country.'

Irene felt a twinge of pain. Why had they spoken to Simon but not to Tom and her? She looked at TJ who dropped his gaze in a manner which hinted at embarrassment.

'There's a new system in the USA, called the Medicare program. It started in 1965. It's a kind of social insurance program to provide health insurance coverage to people who are either age 65 and over, or who meet other special criteria.'

'One slight problem with that might be that you're not 65 and over, and you're not American citizens,' said Irene, still hurt that TJ hadn't come to them to discuss the situation, as well as talking to Simon.

'No, well that's what I was worried about, too,' said Simon. 'But the special criteria is for people who are suffering from illnesses that the American hospitals are keen to learn more about. If that's the case, they will take her and all treatment will be free.'

'And you think that Sophia's blood disorder might be something they are keen to find out more about?' said Tom.

'I wrote to them and asked exactly that. I enclosed her medical information and a letter from the doctor, and I got this back,' said Simon, handing over an envelope. Irene felt another wave of sadness. How long had Simon known?

Inside the envelope was confirmation that the hospital in New York was interested in working with Sophia on a new drug they were developing. The only one of its kind in the world.

'But how would you even do that? TJ would have to give up his job, you would take the kids away from everything they know. And us? We'd be devastated if you were so far away.'

'I know,' said TJ. 'I know, Mum. But if there's a chance of helping Sophia while she's young enough to respond to treatment, we have to go.'

# CHAPTER 13

$\mathcal{L}$et the search begin: Present day

Good God alive, what were we drinking last night? I've woken up this morning in the tiny bed (it says it's a double bed, but I'm not convinced they know who they are dealing with here - Ted and I come to over 40 stone between us).

'Are you awake?' I ask Ted, even though I know he's asleep because I can hear him snoring gently. He's got one of those snuffly snores, not the mad warthog snore that previous boyfriends have had, that you can hear halfway round the M25. No, thank God, Ted has a much gentler noise than that emanating from his open mouth and flared nostrils as he sleeps. I'm not saying it's attractive, but at least it's fairly quiet.

'Ted, Ted,' I repeat. I now seem determined to wake him up for no good reason. It's only 7am, and we haven't arranged to meet the others for breakfast until nine, but I feel the need to chat to him about everything that's been going on.

Eventually the snuffling comes to a sudden stop and he murmurs and opens his eyes, looking over at me all alarmed.

'What happened?' he asks.

'Nothing happened,' I say.

'The car crashed into reception...'

'What are you talking about?'

I thought the car crashed, was that in my dream?'

'It was in your dream,' I say, leaning over and giving him a kiss on the cheek before instantly regretting it when I get a nose full of his garlicky morning breath.

'I had this dream but there was this car full of people that had come swerving off the motorway and crashed into reception.'

'It doesn't take a genius to work out how that dream happened, given the way Melissa was driving that pink van yesterday.'

'I know,' says Ted. 'Can you believe she's never driven more than about five miles in any one trip before, then suddenly she announces she's happy to drive us hundreds of miles across motorways to the south coast? Bloody bonkers.'

There are lots of things that I love very much about Ted, and one of the things I really adore is the way we can chat, and compare notes on what happens.

'Do you think we'll ever find the Gower family?' I ask.

'I think so. With your determination, Melissa's pink van and Simon's driving gloves you can't possibly fail.'

I give him a big hug. 'It's a shame they don't have a more uncommon surname, isn't it?'

'Yes, it might help a bit if they were called the Jabberwocky-

Bockersnappers or something,' he replies, and this amuses me a lot. I howl and snort with laughter in an undignified way and throw myself into his arms and within minutes my clothes are off and we're doing what two people in love tend to do.

'I'm glad I said "Jabberwocky-Bockersnappers,"' Ted reflects, as we lie in bed afterward. 'I might start using that name in daily discourse.'

'It might lose its ability to amuse me if you do that, though.'

He nods, gently, while his eyes start to close, but I'm not having any of it - I want to take us right back to where we were before all the Bockersnapping started...chasing the Gower family.

'I'm glad Sally's coming today - she's quite sensible, and I guess the more of us there are here, the more phoning around and visiting people we can do, then hopefully we will get some positive leads. If we could just find the details for any relations or friends at all, we could pass them on to the private detectives, and make sure the family gets the money that's owing to them.'

'Have you spoken to the private detective firm at all?' asks Ted.

'Yes - I told you. The guy running the firm is really ill. It means we're on our own here. We have to find them.'

Ted smiles broadly as I'm speaking.

'What are you smiling at?'

'You,' he says.

'What have I done that's so funny?'

'Well, you love it, don't you? I know you genuinely want to find them in order to give them the money, but you love things like this. You should've been a bloody private detective. As soon as there's any mystery to solve, you're on it.'

'You're so right. I love things like this. I watch police programmes all the time, and I definitely could solve half the crimes before them.'

Ted and I are first into the breakfast room, and make the most of the rather delicious buffet before the others arrive. It's a continental buffet, which is really the lowest form of hotel buffet, but at least they do fried breakfasts: you have to order them. We decide that we will nibble away on the continental buffet until the others arrive, then make like we've had nothing to eat, and order our breakfasts from the menu.

This is another thing that I dearly love about Ted, he's got the same obsession with hotel breakfast buffets as I have. Or, should I say, he's got the same obsession with food as I have. We try hard not to indulge our every food desire, but we do gain the greatest of pleasures from eating together.

I've just sat down with my second plate of bread rolls, bits of ham, rather rubbery cheese, a small yoghurt, melon and a couple of gherkins and olives, when we see Melissa and Bron-wyn. They are shortly followed by Juan who does a sort of skip and twirl to come and greet us.

'We missed you last night,' I say.

'I should have come, darling, but I really wanted to do the yoga class and it was two hours long. I ended up drinking a couple of gins in the bar here afterward, before crashing out. Then I heard the girls come back, so I joined them for one last drink. Which became several, of course, then I got into a bit of hair dyeing. Do we have a plan for today?'

'We start with the Agricultural College and see what that brings,' I say, as Simon joins us. Melissa shuffles down toward me so he can fit on the table. I notice that she has pink streaks in the front of her hair where once it was auburn.

'We decided to have a little experiment last night,' she says, as she catches me looking. She flicks the pink-tinted strands through her fingers as she speaks. 'Juan did it.'

'It looks nice,' I say. 'Perhaps I should get something like that done, Ted?'

'Please don't,' he says. Then he looks at Melissa. 'It looks fantastic on you, I just don't think it would look that great on Mary.'

'Good save,' I say under my breath and he gives me a mini high-five before I start work on the bread rolls in front of me.

'So, tell me a little bit about who's coming today,' says Melissa. 'Juan was explaining to me last night while I painted his nails, but he wasn't really sure.'

'Her name's Sally,' I say, looking over at Juan's fingernails. They are a deep blackcurrant shade. Quite nice, actually.

'She was at the funeral with her sister, Julie. There was this really awful thing we had to do, right at the end. It was to vote off one of the people who was there, meaning they would get no money. Well, Sally's sister was the one we voted off, because she was really arrogant. I feel guilty about the whole thing, but she wasn't a very nice person, and we were forced to vote or none of us would get any money.

'I felt really sorry for Sally. She tried hard to defend her sister, but Julie was unpleasant. I'm intrigued to see what happened with Julie after the will reading, and how the two of them are now.'

'Me too,' says Simon.

We order our breakfasts, opting for large fry-ups, because we're not entirely sure when we will next be stopping to eat. I

say that, but I'm totally aware that I'm kidding myself, and there
will be plenty of chances to eat throughout the day. There's
really no need to eat a huge breakfast at all, in fact the amount
of food I've had already would be absolutely plenty to keep me
full till lunchtime, but the menu is more than I can resist... the
thought of lovely crispy bacon and scrambled eggs with toma-
toes, mushrooms and sausages...sheer heaven. I place my order
for the largest breakfast they do, ask for a cappuccino and
promise myself that I'll start dieting tomorrow.

'Good Lord alive!' says Simon, utterly transfixed as the waitress lays my plate down on the table.

'It's not that big,' I say, indicating the plate of food
before me.

'Are you not seeing what I'm seeing?' he says.

'Well, yes – it's a big breakfast, but we're not sure when we'll
have lunch.'

'No, not breakfast. Look out through that window and tell
me what you see.'

'Holy mother of God!' I exclaim on seeing the sight of Sally
and Julie walking into the hotel together.

'What is it?' chorus Juan, Melissa and Bronwyn.

'You know we told you about Julie?'

'Yes.'

'Well that rather glamorous woman out there, wiggling
toward the front entrance on sky-high stilettos, is Julie.'

'The one you voted off?'

'Yes.'

'So, she got no money?'

'Yes.'

'So, this is quite embarrassing then?'

'Yes.'

I had forgotten just how beautiful Julie is. Or maybe I just blocked it out of my mind. I remember that she was very attractive, but the vision that walks through the old-fashioned breakfast room, past the tables of elderly diners, all of whom look up wide-eyed at the beauty that has appeared in their midst, is quite magical. She's like a Hollywood movie star, and the whole place seems transformed by her presence. By the time she reaches us, floating gracefully along, in a simple black shift dress, black heels and clutching some designer handbag, the whole room is entranced.

'Hello everyone,' says Sally.

'Surprise! I bet you didn't expect to see me, did you?' says Julie, a smile reaching across her perfect face as she speaks. She is wearing bright red lipstick, and her cat-like eyes are painted in the darkest black. 'Is this really the best hotel you could find? It's like that dreadful place we stayed in for the funeral. What was that place? Half farm, half rundown, dilapidated old building.'

We all just look at her. No one speaks.

'I'm Ted,' says my boyfriend, easing himself up out of his chair and leaning across to shake her hand. She shakes his hand back with a half-smile, looking at him suspiciously. 'Do you work for the hotel?' she asks.

'No, I'm Mary's boyfriend,' he says.

She looks from him to me and I see that smile playing on her lips again. She doesn't comment, but turns to her sister and asks her for a black coffee. Quite why Julie herself can't approach the waitress with the order is a mystery, but she doesn't, just sits down as elegantly as a princess and waits for her sister to do the work for her. Then we all sit in a very uncomfortable silence and wonder how we should proceed.

'I don't know whether you remember me, but I'm Simon,' says our tour leader. He folds away the copy of the *Daily Telegraph* that he's been perusing, and looks up at the two women.

Julie ignores him, but Sally smiles graciously. 'Gosh Simon, of course I know who you are. How are you doing? Everything okay?'

'Everything is great. I'm afraid we've done quite a trek in search of this Gower family, but we know they lived in Southsea, so hopefully we will be able to track them down today.'

'That would be wonderful,' says Sally. 'I'd love to meet them, after all we heard about them. It sounds like they were incredibly kind to Reginald's father.'

'I'm so excited about meeting them,' I say. 'I just can't think about anything else. Can you imagine what it will be like when we see them, standing there, in front of us?'

While we speak of our excitement, Julie sits silently, sipping her coffee, still wearing her sunglasses. She looks around the room imperiously...looking without really seeing, scanning over the people, the furniture and the decor without appearing to take much of it in. Then she turns her attention to me. 'Mary, do you have an address for the Gower family?'

I have just loaded a fork with a huge pile of bacon and eggs and slipped it into my mouth as she asks her question. I masticate wildly, but then lovely Melissa steps in.

'We don't have an address,' says Melissa. 'But this guy in a nursing home in Wales told us that the Gower family moved down here so that's why we are here.'

I have become used to Melissa's garbled voice: her strong Welsh accent and the way she gallops away through sentences. In fact, I have come to think of it as rather endearing. But the look on Julie's face suggests she finds it irritating.

'I don't understand a word of that. Sorry, who are you?'

'I'm Melissa, I was doing Bronny's hair and she is living in the house that the Gower family used to live in like ages ago. And I was there doing the highlights because she needed her roots done and they came and then I knew this guy and he was in a nursing home.'

'Mary, it's a very simple question, do you have an address for the Gower family, or not?' says Julie, cutting off Melissa with her sharp tongue.

Oh God, why did Sally have to bring her horrible sister? And why did the horrible sister make me feel so inadequate, jittery and like I was back in school?

'Are you struggling to understand?' says Ted, rising to his feet. 'It's as if you're simple or something. Melissa just explained that we don't know where they're living yet, and we're here because a guy at a nursing home in Wales, who once knew them, said they had come down here to live. The whole purpose of us being here is to find an address. If you have any clever ideas as to how we might do that, we'd all love to hear them.'

I don't think I've ever been prouder of Ted.

'I wasn't aware that your name was Mary,' says Julie, but I can see that she looks stung by his rebuke. For a second I feel sorry for her. It must be horrible to be so disliked. All the beauty in the world won't win you friends and influence if you're mean and nasty all the time.

'No, my name is Ted. But when you're rude and aggressive to Mary it'll be me who answers you.'

I love Ted for intervening in heroic fashion, but I've never needed anyone to answer for me and I slightly resent his claim that he will be replying on my behalf from now on.

I'm also well aware that if we sit here fighting and back-talking one another, we will never find the Gower family.

'Okay, let's try and put all this behind us, and focus, shall we?' I say, like a frustrated teacher of misbehaving teenagers.

'Yes, goodness, yes,' says Simon. 'We have so much to do, let's all try and get on, please.'

'Okay. Well, the starting point is obviously the Agricultural College. I was thinking last night that maybe we could look in local newspaper cuttings for any stories. I wonder whether local newspapers are online. That would definitely be worth checking.'

As I speak, I see Melissa and Bronwyn pick up their phones. It's a matter of minutes before they tell me that many of the archives of the *Portsmouth News* are online, so I put them in charge of finding any mentions of Tom or Irene Gower.

Julie stays silent through the whole exchange, then she asks one simple question which answers all my questions about why she's come to Southsea to join the search.

'Is Mike coming?' she asks.

Until she mentioned him, I'd forgotten about Julie's fascination with Mike Sween - the really handsome SKY TV guy, who had been at the funeral. She and Mike had been all over each other. I have no idea whether they are still together, or have even seen each other since. Clearly, she still holds a torch for him.

'I don't think so, Julie. He's not really responded to the various messages.'

'I'll drop him a text, and see whether I can motivate him to come.'

'Great,' I say.

# CHAPTER 14

## *A* Day at College: Present day

We all bundle into Melissa's hairdressing van (I say 'all of us' - Julie insisted on taking a cab), and head the short distance to Highbury, a small borough in Portsmouth to the college.

Despite our best efforts to put Simon in the driving seat, Melissa insists on taking the wheel and driving like a woman possessed through the streets of Portsmouth. There's something paradoxical about being in a vehicle with a recklessly fast driver, because whilst you're driving at the speed of light and not really stopping at red lights and junctions, and thus reach your destination more quickly, the whole thing feels much longer because you're experiencing every second that passes with such morbid dread, that every second lasts a lifetime.

By the time we reach the college, I am 94-years-old.

'Hello,' I say to the austere-looking woman on reception. 'I don't know whether you can help me but I'm desperately trying to track down a man who was a lecturer at Portsmouth Agricultural College in the 60s and 70s.'

There is a long silence and I think she's going to tell me she can't help.

'We have an extensive library department here, but all records are stored on microfiche. I'm afraid they haven't been transferred onto the computers, so it's a bit of a laborious task, but you're welcome to come in and look through.'

'That would be brilliant,' I say. 'Can we come now?'

'Yes, let me book you in. What's your name?'

'Mary Brown,' I say, before explaining to her that, ideally, eight of us would like to come.

'The most we can take is two,' she says. 'I'm afraid the microfiche is only available on one computer, so only two people can sit at it.'

'Okay then, can you put my name down and the other name is Simon Blake.'

'All done,' she says, handing me two lanyards.

I think there might be a little bit of quibbling when I tell the others that only two people can be in the microfiche department at any one time, and that I have given mine and Simon's names, but it seems that looking through old microfiche in the stuffy old library of a remote agricultural college isn't what most people think of as great fun, so they are quite happy to let Simon and me do the task.

'Darling, I will be looking around all the boutiques in the local town,' says Juan. 'Old Portsmouth has nice shops, according to the lady on reception in the hotel. I need new sequined dancing tights.'

'No, you don't,' I say.

'I do,' he responds.

'You wouldn't want to get yourself some nice jeans or jogging bottoms instead?'

'Nope.'

'I'll be in the pub having pie and chips and a sneaky pint if anyone wants to join me,' says Ted.

There are no takers. To be honest, Ted looks relieved. Simon and I leave them to it and walk toward the college.

'Wait for us two before having lunch, won't you?' I say to Ted. 'Then Simon and I can give you all the feedback as we eat.'

'Sure,' says Ted, in a way that indicates that he has every intention of having the biggest lunch he can get his hands on. Even though we've just enjoyed a huge cooked breakfast.

Walking into the college is an astonishing experience. Have you been into a college or university recently? I haven't. I walk into the library expecting it to be a bit like school, but inside it's more like a business… All very formal and sensibly set out, with our pass cards needed to get past all the security systems, and all these employees who look as if they're working in Deutsche Bank or something.

We go through to the small area at the back of the library where the computer terminals sit. The microfiche machine is very old-fashioned looking compared to the rest of the library, and clearly doesn't get much use by the students. It has a tatty note Sellotaped on the top saying 'microfiche only'.

A kindly librarian assists us in operating the machine, and pulls up the slides from 1960.

That's when I realise what a massive undertaking this is. There are tonnes of slides. 'We might be here for weeks,' I say to Simon.

'I hope to goodness he didn't start work at this college in 1970 or something,' he replies. 'It's going to take us forever to get through each week, never mind having to go through decades.'

'We definitely should have brought snacks.'

'I'm sure we'll survive.'

The microfiche slides contain the college newsletters, or 'bulletins' as they call them. I scan through, desperately looking for the name 'Tom Gower'.

After two hours of searching, Simon and I are beginning to despair when I spot his name.

'The college is pleased to welcome Mr. Tom Gower,' I shriek.

'Oh, finally,' says Simon, in a more muted voice.

'It says that Tom will be a lecturer in the agriculture department, teaching first-year students the basics of dairy farming. Tom is a former farmer himself, so I'm sure he will have lots of information and experience to pass on to our students. We wish him all the best.'

Simon looms over me to get a better look at the screen, and for some reason I think he's going to give me a high-five, so I put out my hand, but he just looks at me and I feel a complete fool, so I drop my hand back down and turn back to the microfiche.

Tom Gower started here in 1960. Great. But what does that mean? How is that relevant to where he is now?

'You know what we're going to have to do, don't you?' I say to Simon.

'I was thinking exactly the same thing,' said Simon. 'Knowing when he started is interesting, but not especially useful. We're going to have to find out when he left, and hope it says where he went after leaving.'

'But it won't say that. These are school bulletins. They are only going to say they are sorry to see him go.'

'It might say: 'We wish him well at Bath College' or something.'

'That's true,' I say.

And so we turn our attention back to the microfiche and go in search of Tom Gower. We read and read and flick through the slides and read some more. Hours are passing, darkness is descending outside. I am becoming irritated and annoyed that the others are all out shopping, drinking and enjoying themselves and I am stuck in here. Then I remind myself that this was my choice. I wanted to be here, in the thick of it.

So I carry on reading.

The two of us are dizzy and frustrated before we finally find it, in a bulletin sent in 1969, announcing that Mr. Tom Gower will be retiring from his position as head of agriculture.

'Ooooooo,' we chorus. 'Head of Agriculture. He had a few promotions along the way.'

Then, joy of joys, a picture of Mr. Gower, with his wife Irene.

'Oh my God - look how beautiful she is. Gosh, I didn't imagine her looking like that.'

'Read here,' says Simon, pointing to the text on the screen. It says she's been working at Grant's Estate Agents.'

We take pictures of everything we've found, clicking away at the screen in order to capture the information.

'All dates, and all names,' I say. 'We might have to contact some of the other people who were working there at the time, make sure you have their names.'

Simon clicks away on his camera, like he is the paparazzi.

'I've got everything,' he says, as we switch off the computer, pile all the microfiche tapes together, and head out of the library.

It's 4pm when we walk out into the natural light and almost flinch from the intensity of it. Like that feeling you get when you walk out of the cinema in the middle of the day, and are astonished to find it light outside.

'We've got a bit of research to do, haven't we?' I say to Simon, as we stand there, breathing in the fresh air and mulling over our options.

'Let's go to the estate agents,' he says, decisively.

He seems more engaged with the process now, which cheers me no end. I thought it was me against the world in the battle to find the Gowers.

I google Grants Estate Agents and discover it's still operating and based not too far away, just a little further along the seafront, so I message the group to tell them to meet us there.

'Estate agents? You and Simon have decided to buy a house together here, have you?' asks Ted.

'Ha, ha. It's where Irene Gower worked.'

'Oooooo,' says Ted. 'I'll see you there.'


The estate agents looks shabby, to be honest. It has a rundown appearance, as if it hasn't quite moved into the 21st century. Other estate agents nearby have glossy exteriors, with screens in the windows, flicking between different houses that are for sale. In Grant's Estate Agent's window there's a collection of small cards, barely bigger than postcards with pictures of houses on them. The paint around the windows is peeling and in an unattractive moss-green colour.

Why would they allow that to happen when it's next to sparkling white, clean and elegant rival firms? There's no way anyone would ever choose to go in this one rather than the others.

I push the door open and see the surprise on the face of the young woman sitting there, as if confirming my thoughts about the place. What if Irene still works here? This could be her daughter. They might have had another child after Tom Junior.

'Sorry to disturb you, but I'm looking for Irene Gower,' I say. 'She used to work here.'

'Sorry, I don't know anyone by that name,' says the woman.

'Would you have any records, by any chance, of staff who worked here in, like, the 1960s and 70s?'

'The 60s and 70s? I don't think we've been here that long.'

'Is there any way you could find out?'

'The agency is owned by a guy called Gary Grant. I could call him?'

'Yes please.'

The receptionist rings her boss, and we all stand there in silence as she asks him whether he's ever heard of Irene Gower.

'He wants to talk to you,' she says, handing over her mobile phone.

'My name's Gary, I'm the owner of the business. Can I ask why you want to know?' he says.

'I'm trying to track down Irene Gower,' I say. 'She worked at this company in the late 60s.'

'Who are you? Are you related to her?'

'No. It's a really complicated story, but she was very kind to a man once. The man's son passed away a year ago and left a lot of money. He wanted to let her have a fairly big amount of it, but no one can find her and her husband. I was also left money, and I just want to find her, so the money can be passed on. We're a bit short on information, but we know she worked at the estate agents, and wondered whether you might be able to help?'

'Right.'

'Do you think you might be able to?'

'My grandpa used to own the estate agents. He definitely knew Irene.'

'Oh good. I'd like to visit her.'

'Heavens, she'd be over a hundred years old by now. I don't imagine she's still alive.'

'Yes - sorry - I mean do you know where any of her descendants might be? Do you know her son TJ?'

'Look, I never knew her. I just know that she worked here and that she broke my grandpa's heart and ruined his life.'

'What?'

'My grandpa was infatuated with her. When he died, twenty years ago, we found letters they were sending to one another, long after she'd moved away.'

'Are you sure? She was married, though. To Tom Gower.'

'I'm sure.'

'And do you know where they moved?'

'To Brighton,' he said. 'In the letters my grandpa is asking her whether she moved there to get away from him. She replied that she moved there because her son and grandchild were living there.'

'Do you know if she's still living in Brighton?'

'No idea. In one of the letters, she encloses a picture that her husband drew of her, and mentions that he's been doing cartoons for the *Brighton Argus*. That's all I know, I'm afraid. I can't say I'm very impressed with a woman who gets her husband to draw her, then sends it to another man, but - there you go. Nothing I've heard about that woman impresses me much.'

'Thank you so much for your time, you've been really help-ful,' I tell Gary.

I don't like the way he talks about Irene...I feel strangely attached to the Gower family, and quite defensive of them, but she does sound like a right old minx.

'They are in Brighton,' I say, as we leave the estate agents. I've decided not to share the romantic entanglements of our target with them all just yet. I don't want them to be put off her, and decide they want to end the search. 'Tom was working for the *Brighton Argus*. Might be worth going to Brighton?'

'Well, phone them first, Mary. I'd rather not subject myself to another long journey unless it's absolutely necessary,' says Simon.

'Of course,' I reply. Why isn't anyone else as ridiculously excited by all this as I am? I want to get straight on the road and off to Brighton. Instead, I dial the number for the *Brighton Argus*.

'Hello, my name's Mary Brown. I wonder whether I could talk to someone who deals with the cartoonists on the paper, please.'

'Can you let me know what it's to do with?'

'Well, it's a bit complicated, but I am trying to track down a cartoonist who worked on the paper many years ago. Or, rather, I'm trying to track down his family. I just wondered whether there was anyone on the paper still in touch with him or his family who could help me.'

'Right,' says the receptionist, with very little confidence in her voice. 'I'll put you through to the art desk, and someone there might be able to help.'

'Hello, Sandra speaking,' come the dulcet tones of someone with a very strong Essex accent. I go through the rigmarole of explaining what I'm after, and wait for a couple of seconds while she clearly thinks about how to get rid of me.

'Have you checked our site online to see whether he's still here?' she says.

'No, he's definitely not still there, I didn't know whether anyone working there now had stayed in touch with him after he left.'

'Hang on one second,' she says. 'Could you tell me what the name was again?'

'Tom Gower.'

She disappears from the line and I prepare myself for the news that no one at the newspaper remembers him, but instead - she has an idea. She tells me that my best bet would be to talk to Russell Clow. He is retired now, but started work on the paper when he was 18, back in the late 60s, and he worked for the paper all his life until retiring six or seven years ago.

'Can I take your number, and I'll ring him and see whether he's willing to talk to you?'

It's only 20 minutes later when the phone rings, and she tells me that Russell Clow remembers Tom Gower very clearly, and he's happy to meet me in the morning if I want to come to the *Brighton Argus* offices.

I give a squeal of delight at this point, and say that I would love to come and meet him. 'I'll come to the offices at 11am in the morning.'

'Eleven am in the morning?' says Simon, who's been overhearing the call. 'I think we've done quite enough trekking across the country, haven't we? I suggest we have a look round Southsea, then head back to Wales tomorrow. We've tried our best. We can't keep going like this.'

'No - we have to go to Brighton,' I say. 'We have to.'

'No, come on, Mary, enough is enough,' says Ted.

But I know I can win him round again.

*Mysterious Invitation WhatsApp Group*

**Mary Brown**

Hi everyone… Guess what? We're off again! We are heading to Brighton, because we've discovered that's where they moved after Southsea. Anyone coming to join us?

**Mike Sween**

Yeah, I'll come down for a couple of days. Where will you be staying?

**Julie Bramley**

Hey you, looking forward to seeing you tomorrow. If you want to come tonight instead, I'm free for dinner. xx

**Mike Sween**

I can't make it til the morning, but look forward to seeing you all around 10.30am.

. . .

**Simon Blake**

I've just booked us all into the Holiday Inn on Brighton Seafront

**Mary Brown**

Hey Mike - looking forward to seeing you tomorrow. PS Holiday Inn on the seafront looks better in the brochure than it sounds!

**Mike Sween**

Ha, ha. Thanks Mary. That's a relief!

**Julie Bramley**

And if you do decide to come down tonight, my offer of dinner still stands... much love xxx

# CHAPTER 15

*B*righton Bound: Present Day

Early the next morning, we all climb into the pink hairdressing van. The luggage is piled into the tiny boot which isn't really a boot at all so it spills over into the back so it's all lying next to us.

'This is cosy, isn't it?' says Sally, rather understating things, as we sit down, all squashed up next to one another. Julie comes with us in the van, which is remarkable. I fully expect her to call a chauffeur-driven car, or have unicorns summoned to fly her there, but in the end she decides to honour us with her presence. She snags the only single seat, so she isn't shoved up against anyone else, and sits in splendid isolation, looking remote and judgmental as the van winds its way through Southsea and off toward Brighton.

Julie is completely overdressed, as we knew she would be given Mike will be waiting for us when we get to the hotel. She wears a fitted purple dress, sky-high cream pumps and her cream coat draped over her shoulders without putting her arms into it. This is something that no one in real life ever does. It's only TV presenters and models on those fashion slots on *This Morning* who wear coats like capes. The rest of us normal human beings would spend our entire days picking them up off the floor if we did that. Julie doesn't, of course, but then she could hardly be described as 'normal' with her ridiculously pretty face, gorgeous hair, and ankles the width of a pencil.

'Will it take long?' she asks, like a petulant five-year-old, before returning to study her phone.

'It takes about an hour and a quarter, depending on the traffic,' says Simon knowledgeably. 'But the route takes us along the seafront all the way so it should be a very pleasant trip.'

'Gosh, yes, because staring at the sea for over an hour is exactly what I want to do first thing in the morning.'

I pull my notebook out of my bag and start to jot down some thoughts, listing the questions I need to ask of Russell when we get to the *Brighton Argus*.

When did Tom work for the *Brighton Argus*?

Why did he leave? What did he go on to do next?

His address?

Any close friends who might still be in touch with the family?

TJ. What about him? Did he marry? What's his wife's name? Can we track her down?

'We'll head to the hotel first, shall we?' says Simon, looking over my shoulder, and seeing the notes I am scribbling on my pad.

'Yes. Let's go there, drop everything off, and have a chat, to make sure we know exactly what we want to find out, then head for the *Brighton Argus* at 11am. I hope they are still living in this area.'

'You realise that Irene and Tom Gower are most likely dead, and their children will be quite old by now.'

'Yes. I know. I'm thinking of the children and grandchildren. It would be great to find them.'

'The children could well be in the area. They moved around so much, they might well want to settle somewhere and put some roots down. I wonder whether people are less inclined to move around when they're old. I guess one gets to the stage when one just stays where one is? I certainly feel like I'm approaching that stage of life myself.'

'I know what you mean,' I reply, sagely. 'And it would certainly be very handy for us if they still lived in the Brighton area.'

'Very much so,' says Simon, tapping his nose conspiratorially. I've no idea why he does that.

The van winds its way through the narrow, pretty streets just off the seafront, until it comes to a standstill next to a big hotel. I'm not a fan of these huge corporate hotels. I much prefer a little, country hotel. But it is cheap, looks nice on the website, and is well-located for the newspaper headquarters situated in the next street. Also, we don't know the area, and this place looks as good as any other.

We walk into the hotel reception and I'm aware straight away that Mike is here because of the change in Julie. She fusses with her hair and smooths down her dress and looks for all the world like a woman on a mission. Whatever else happens in Brighton, at least we'll have the joy of watching Julie pursue Mike in the hope of rekindling the romance they shared in Wales.

Sure enough, he is there in the reception area, ready to meet us when we walk in. He's tall, tanned and handsome in jeans, a white shirt and a cream linen jacket with a flash of foppish blue handkerchief emerging from his top pocket. He is really very handsome. His hair is longer than it was before. It lends him an English gentleman air, kind of like Hugh Grant in *Four Weddings and a Funeral*, but bigger and more head turning. 'Oh darling,' declares Julie, wiggling her way up to him and kissing him on the cheek. 'You look absolutely gorgeous. How have you been?' She's standing very close to him and stroking his arm as she speaks. Next to him is a woman from the hotel. She's dressed in a knee-length navy skirt that looks two sizes too big for her, a white jumper that is pulled down over her hands in that really annoying way, thick tights and flat, black shoes. She looks like every receptionist ever.

We all pile up to him and hug him and say how pleased we are that he's here.

'We'll have to update you on everything that's happened. It's been quite a journey,' I tell him, and he smiles warmly and gives me a big hug.

'It's so nice to see you, Mary. I'm dying to hear all about what you've been up to. Now there's someone I need to introduce you to.' He steps to one side, and introduces the hotel receptionist lady.

'This is Polly,' he says. I shake hands with her and tell her what a nice hotel it is. She looks quite surprised by this. Then I introduce Ted, and Juan.

'How long have you worked here?' I ask.

'No, Polly is my girlfriend.'

Now I can't begin to explain to you the look that crosses the delicate features of our supermodel friend when Mike makes this unlikely announcement. Julie looks distraught and horrified in equal measure. I'm not sure whether she's more worried about the fact that he's brought a girlfriend with him, or that the girlfriend is so plain. I don't mean to be mean, but Polly really is a 100 percent girl next door, with her mousy blonde hair and sensible clothes. She appears to have a very slim figure, but she's drowned in the skirt and loose-fitting jumper. She isn't wearing a scrap of makeup, unlike Julie who is painted thickly with the stuff, and looks like she's stepped off the cover of *Vogue*.

'Your girlfriend?' she says.

'Yes, my girlfriend.'

Julie laughs, turns and walks away.

We stand there in stunned silence.

I'm about to say something like 'thank you for coming' or 'let me tell you what we've been up to' to fill the emptiness caused by Julie's sudden departure when the click-clack of heels in the foyer informs us that she is on the way back.

She charges along without any of the hip swaying, chin-raising haughtiness that she usually displays.

'Really, Mike? Really?' she shouts at him.

'Yes, she's really my girlfriend,' Mike says. 'Her name is Polly and she works at SKY, don't you sweetheart?'

Polly nods, looking a little confused and unaware of why she's provoked this reaction in Julie.

'You're at SKY, are you?' says Julie. 'Goodness me. Not on screen I imagine?'

I see Mike's eyes narrow. 'What do you mean by that?'

'Let's be honest, Mike. She doesn't look like a TV star. Does she?'

'Thank goodness, she doesn't. She looks lovely and natural and attractive. She's an incredibly kind, sweet person. And we're very much in love.'

I watch as Julie's eyes darken, and wish someone would come along with popcorn. This is likely to be quite a scene.

'Did you know that Mike and I had a brief fling?' Julie says.

Polly continues to look baffled by everything.

'I didn't know that,' she says, with a beautiful voice.

I'm dying to tell her what a lovely voice she has, but decide not to intervene at this juncture.

'Yes. We had a very steamy passionate fling. It was momentous.'

'Oh, for goodness sake, Julie. We spent one night together over a year ago.' He puts his arm around Polly and pulls her in close to him.

'I could have any man I want. But I thought that you and I had something special.'

'Julie, we had one night together. A year ago. This is all very embarrassing and making Polly feel uncomfortable.'

'So what does 'Polly' do at SKY then?' Julie asks, for some reason she makes quotation marks in the air as she says Polly's name. 'Does she make the tea or something?'

'I do voice overs, programme announcements and links between programmes. I also do quite a lot of voiceovers for films.' Polly seems to be gaining some confidence. And that voice of hers is quite lovely.

'I can see why you'd do voice over work. You have a beautiful voice,' I say.

Julie laughs. 'I thought you were going to say that you can see why she does voice overs - because she's too ugly to be on screen. That would be nearer the truth.'

'How dare you?' Mike says so loud that I jump a little and take a step back. 'If you were a man, I'd hit you.'

'Now come on,' says Ted, stepping between them. 'This is getting ridiculous. Everyone needs to calm down. Julie - why don't you go to your room, and let's all catch up for lunch later, shall we?'

This seems like a reasonable suggestion, but Julie's having none of it.

'You are crazy,' she shouts. 'Absolutely crazy. You could have had me, and you've gone for her instead.'

'I did have you,' said Mike. 'And it wasn't up to much. I've met someone here that I love desperately. I want to spend the rest of my life with her. I hope you meet someone that you feel similarly about, one day. Until that day, keep away from me, and particularly keep away from Polly and let's all get through the next few days in as dignified a way as possible.'

'You're a fool,' barks Julie, but I can hear a slight crack in her voice, giving away how upset she is about all this. Then she stomps off in the direction of the lift. She has left her bag behind, with her key lying on top of it. I realise she's going to have to stomp back and pick them up. Despite disliking her intensely, I feel a wave of warmth toward her. I don't want her to have to go through that humiliation. So, I pick up her key and her bag and run after her, handing them to her. She gives me a look of tenderness that I've never seen in her face before. Her eyes are full of tears, and I long to hug her, but I'm scared of how she'll react, so I back off and re-join the group. Ted hugs me and kisses me lightly on my forehead.

'Well done, sweetheart,' he says, 'That was a very kind thing to do.'

'Well,' says Simon, when the lift has taken Julie out of earshot. 'That was all a bit dramatic, but welcome all the same, Polly. The rest of us are very happy to see you.'

'Thank you,' she says.

I glance at my watch while everyone collects their bags and makes arrangements to meet in the dining room later. It's much later than I thought it was.

'We have an appointment at the *Brighton Argus* in 20 minutes,' I say to Simon. 'Are you ready?'

'I'll be five minutes,' he says. 'I just have to visit the little boys' room.'

I kiss Ted on the cheek before we leave, then text him while we're walking to the newspaper. 'Make sure you send full reports on everything going on there. I need to know what happens, how mad Julie goes, and whether Polly ever cracks and punches her...'

'You can count on me,' he texts back.

The *Brighton Argus* buzzes with life and activity. I thought local newspapers were sleepy. Not this place. Journalists rush around and clocks on the wall indicate the time in New York, Los Angeles, and London. I'm struggling to see why they need to know the time anywhere but Brighton, but still, it gives the place an air of importance and an aura of discipline, hard work and creativity.

It also gives me a strange confidence in our ability to find out all about Tom Gower.

We're standing at the entrance to the impressive newsroom when I see an elderly man lift himself out of his seat on the far side of the news desk and walk over to us, smiling and welcoming.

'I'm Russell,' he says.

'Oh, nice to meet you. My name's Mary, and this is Simon.' We all shake hands, and he invites us to a small studio which has been setup with a couple of microphones and a green screen.

'Are we going to make a show?' I say, lightly.

'No. This used to be a meeting room, obviously they do all sorts of high-tech nonsense in here now. Just ignore all the stuff.'

'So, you do TV and radio recordings here?'

'Not me. I retired years ago, but the website has lots of videos on it, so I guess this is where they record them. Now, what can I do for you?'

'Okay. This is very complicated, so bear with me.' I tell him the story of the funeral, and the money and the fact that the Gower family were missing, and how much Reginald had wanted the money to go to Tom's descendants as a gesture of thanks for how kind they had been to his father.

'That's good to hear,' says Russell. 'Tom was a very decent man. Too decent in a way.'

'How?'

'Well, he would have made a much better cartoonist if he'd been more aggressive, spikier. His drawings were good, and his ideas were good, but he never pushed things far enough to make people gasp.'

'Gosh, that's really interesting. So, he wasn't nasty enough?'

'Well - it's not that you have to be nasty, but you need an edge.'

'Oh, okay. Did you work with Tom much?'

'Yes, I was a runner for the photographers; taking their films back to the offices after they'd shot them. These were the days way before digital cameras so every photographer would have a runner who'd get the films back to the office ready to be processed. I had moved to the art desk by the time Tom started. I guess he'd have been in his mid-50s. And I was about 21. I was his assistant.

'He wasn't based in the office, but he submitted cartoons. I used to cycle to his house to get them and bring them in here. He was a lovely chap. He had a very beautiful wife as I remember. Yes, Irene. I say, she was very beautiful. I think they had some relationship problems, though, didn't they?'

'Oh, did they? That's interesting. I thought maybe they had. We talked to a guy in Southsea who worked at the estate agents where she used to work. He said his grandpa and her had this thing going.'

'The estate agent. Yes, my goodness. I remember something about that. Mark was his name, wasn't it? Tom used to mention him. He said he was glad they were away from Southsea, but he always wondered whether Irene was still in touch with Mark. I don't know whether they were actually having an affair or not, but it was something that always played on Tom's mind.'

'Do you know what happened to him after he left?'

'After America, you mean?'

'I meant after he left the *Brighton Argus*.'

'Oh, I see. The last I heard was that the whole family was in the USA.'

Simon and I stand there in sombre silence, grimly realising that there is no way we'll find the family now.

'Are his grandchildren still in the USA?'

'I don't know. I never knew much about the grandchildren, they were very little when he was working for us. The younger grandchild had an illness that they were all very worried about, and there was a treatment being developed at a hospital in New York. They went out there to be a test case. We kept in touch for a while. But then lost touch, as is always the case.

'He said that the treatment had worked well. As far as I can remember. I mean, I don't suppose this is any use to you at all, is it?'

'It's very useful,' I say. 'I had hoped that the family might still be living around here, but knowing they are not, and are not even in the country, has saved us a lot of time.'

'I'm so sorry I can't be any more help. They all settled in New York. I mean the grandchildren would be all grown up by now, wouldn't they? They probably have children of their own.'

'Yes, they would. Well, thank you for your time.'

'No problem at all,' he says. 'Just a thought - but I'll look up the name of the illness the little girl had, and the name of the hospital they went to in New York. If you can't find them, and the money is just sitting there, you could donate it to them. He felt passionately about everything the hospital was doing.'

'Thanks, yes, that would be great,' I say. 'Then we can put all of that to the private detectives and know that the money is somewhere Tom and Irene would have approved.'

. . .

Simon and I walk back to the hotel in silence. I feel like I've been beaten up. There's no way we'll find them now. At lunch everyone asks me to update them on the situation.

'Okay,' I say, standing up and shrugging my shoulders. 'Tom and Irene Gower did live in Brighton, and it sounds like he made a real success of it as a cartoonist, but the family upped and left and went off to live in America.'

There's a huge groan from the group at this point.

'I know. I am really disappointed too. But Russell, the guy on the newspaper in Brighton who knew Tom, said that his grandchild had a blood disorder and they went to the USA because there was a hospital in New York who offered to try and help. Then they settled there.'

Later that night, I tell Ted everything, about the estate agent telling me about the affair, and Russell all but confirming it. Then I sit on the edge of the bed to take my eye makeup off.

'I can't believe we won't find them,' I say, embarrassingly close to tears. Ted wraps his arms around me and pulls me into him. 'I feel so sad. I feel really sad for Tom. If Irene had an affair and he knew about it, it must have been awful.'

'We don't know that he knew about it. He might have thought they were happy together.'

'I guess, but people tend to, don't they? I bet he did know. It must have been awful for him. And their grandchildren getting sick and having to go over to New York. That must have been so hard.'

'Yes. New York in the 60s and 70s wasn't like it is today. It would have all been quite a change from working on the farm in Gower.'

And that's when I burst into tears...crying big, fat, ugly tears into my boyfriend's shirt.

'Come on, sweetheart, we've done everything we can. You've been amazing, but we can't go over to New York.'

'Can't we?'

'No.'

# CHAPTER 16

*F*ears for Simon: 1978

Irene handed the last of the dishes to Tom, and plunged her hands back into the soapy water to pull out the plug. Tom seemed lost in a world of his own as he dried the bowl and put it into the cupboard.

They'd reached a comfortable place in their lives, living together in some sort of harmony after all the disruptions. She still spoke to Mark occasionally, but she suspected that he'd moved on and met someone else. The calls they shared were fewer these days and her memories of him - though still warming and plentiful, were definitely dimmed by time.

'I must call TJ later,' she said to her husband, as she wiped around the sink and threw the cloth across the taps to dry. 'Did you know they have been in New York for five years now? It was five years ago today that they left. Can you believe that? Sophia is eight-years-old. It's crazy how time flies.'

'It's crazy but they've done so well - all set up, and with Sophia having responded to the drugs. I'm proud of them.'

Irene smiled as if to agree with her husband, while walking into the sitting room to make the trans-Atlantic call. She was absolutely thrilled that everything was working out for them, but devastated that they had decided to stay in New York, rather than come home. She felt as if she wasn't part of their lives, and was missing seeing the grandchildren grow up. Then, there was Simon. She didn't know how much to tell them, but Simon was very unwell. He had a leaky heart valve that required a complicated operation. He'd urged Irene not to mention it to Yvonne and TJ, but it was difficult. She felt bad for not telling them.

TJ picked up the phone in New York and realised straight away that it was his mother calling...that familiar long-distance hum that preceded her words. The faltering speech and the endless wait for her to respond to a question. The phone calls home were always very difficult. Not so much now that they were all settled in, but to start with it had been a real problem to keep the conversations with his mother light and chatty.

He hadn't wanted to burden her with any of his problems, but the truth was that New York had not proven to be the easiest place to settle into when he and the family had first arrived on that dark winter's evening five years ago, clutching their young children and wondering whether they had done the right thing.

They had feared for themselves in a city that they'd been

warned was dirty and dangerous...traipsing bags and cases onto buses, and avoiding the underground as they found their way to their Manhattan apartment.

They had been worried about so much. Were they wise to give Sophia drugs that were not approved and still in the experimental stage? Should he have left his job? Would they ever fit in?

He never wanted to share any of his fears with his mother, so he'd keep the conversation light and tell her about the magnificence of the huge building in which he now worked, and how well he was doing.

As they chatted on this occasion, it was Irene keeping things light, avoiding talk of Simon, and hoping that he may recover without needing surgery, hoping the doctors had got the prognosis wrong. When TJ asked about Simon, she said that he was very tired, but otherwise seemed well. Then she came off the phone and thought long and hard about whether she'd done the right thing. Shouldn't she just tell the truth?

Six months after the phone call, it was Tom, not Irene, who phoned to break the news: Simon had gone in to surgery for a double heart by-pass and to fix a leaky valve.

A week later, Tom was forced to ring again to tell TJ that he would be wise to come back, as Simon was drifting in and out of consciousness and might not recover.

The days after the phone call were spent in a blur of hoping and praying that Yvonne and TJ would arrive back before Simon died.

They did.

Just.

Whether by force of sheer will or by luck, Simon clung to life until his daughter and her family returned from New York. He was able to smile at them as they came in to see him, and squeeze his daughter's hand one last time before slipping away.

# CHAPTER 17

## The end of love 1990

They all sat around the table, smiling, laughing and hoping that Tom understood what was happening. Irene put the birthday cake down on the table in front of him. It was a superman cake, as he had requested, and had a collection of candles on the top. Not the 75 that would have been required to match his age, but lots of them, all flickering brightly.

'Blow them out, dad,' said TJ, putting his arm gently around his dad's shoulder, with such affection that Irene felt a rise of warmth inside her. She loved them both so much.

Tom looked blankly at the cake in front of him, then put his arm out, into the flames of the candles. TJ reached over to pull his arm out of danger's way, while Yvonne pulled the cake back.

Tom stared at his shirt where the cuff was burned, leaving a scorched mark.

'Shall we get you to bed now,' said Irene, moving round to her husband's side, and checking the burned cuff to make sure there wasn't a burned wrist beneath it.

'Bedtime,' said Tom standing up. He was being far more cooperative than he usually was. Perhaps he was tired? Perhaps the smell of burning had scared him? Who knew? It was impossible to know how he was feeling for vast swathes of time. On other occasions, he'd scream at everyone and tell them exactly how he felt and what he thought of them.

'Sophia, can you put down the magazine and go and help your mother,' said Irene, as she led Tom upstairs. She was tired and fed up, and could see Yvonne rushing around to tidy the place up, while an 18-year-old who should know better, slumped in the corner to check the new fashions in her weekly magazine.

'Come on, Tom. Up we go, one step at a time.'

By the time she'd got her husband to sleep, and come back downstairs, she was grateful for the tidied room and large drink waiting for her on the kitchen table.

She sat down next to her son, Yvonne and her grandson Andrew. Sophia sat in the sitting room, talking on the phone, Irene's phone, while chewing gum. Irene hated to complain about her all the time, but by the time Irene was 18, she was out working. At least Andrew showed interest in the family, and was helpful and kind. He'd recently graduated from university and was applying for jobs. No one seemed to have any expectations of Sophia, and it drove Irene nuts. What sort of 18-year-old comes round to her grandparents' place to visit her very sick grandfather, then picks up the phone and starts calling her friends, without even asking whether she can use the phone?

Jane most definitely would not have approved of her grand-daughter's slovenly ways.

'What are we going to do?' said TJ, taking his mother's hands.

'Make her help around the house more. Insist she gets a job. There are lots of things you could do.'

'No, not Sophia,' said Yvonne, who had begun to despair of the way in which Irene treated Sophia, expecting her to do so much more around the house because she was a girl. It was 1990, not the 1950s.

'I meant Dad,' said TJ, being much gentler with his mother than Yvonne felt inclined to be.

'There's nothing we can do. I'll look after him.'

'But, Mum, that's so difficult. It's okay when we're all here to help, but when you're on your own you can't possibly be expected to watch him all the time. He nearly set fire to himself just then, and that's with us all sitting around. He's going to hurt himself. We have to think about putting him in a home.'

'Absolutely not,' said Irene. 'No way on earth am I dumping him when he's at his most vulnerable. I will look after him. Perhaps Sophia could come over here and help me, from time to time?'

Yvonne stood up and walked away, over to the kettle in the corner of the room. She had no intention of making coffee: she just needed to remove herself from the conversation.

'Will you at least think about putting him into care, Mum? It could be better for all of us. Dad most of all,' said TJ.

'I have thought about it, and have decided not to.'

Irene's reluctance to confine her husband to a home was

motivated by a deep-seated love for the man she married when barely out of her teens, and also a splinter of guilt. She'd put him through so much pain. Now, when he really needed her, when they were in a foreign country, so far from the life he had been born into, she would look after him, as he had looked after and tolerated her so many times.

They had come to New York to look after their family, now the family needed to look after them. That's how the world worked, and Irene felt angry and frustrated with Yvonne for not wanting any pressures on her own family, and for wanting Tom's problems confined to a discreet home on the other side of town. Well, that wouldn't be happening.

'Your father would have sacrificed everything he has, and everything he is, for you,' she said, doing nothing to hide the bitterness she felt. 'He's desperately ill and in need of help. Now we will give everything for him.'

TJ put his arms around his mother. 'Of course, we will, Mum. Of course. We'll make sure everyone is involved in coming over and helping with everything.'

'Thank you,' she said. 'It's the least we can all do. If you could come over and just spend time with him, talking to him, it would make the world of difference,' she said, addressing her comments to the whole room, but meaning them mostly for Yvonne and Sophie who always seemed so indulged and selfish.

TJ promised that everyone would help, and Irene excused herself and headed upstairs to sit by Tom. She hated what dementia had done to him: stolen everything from him - his abilities and all his senses. Worst of all - his memories. He could remember things from long ago, and spoke frequently about the farm, asking whether Marco was coping okay, and whether the cows had been milked, but he remembered nothing of the things they were doing in the present day.

Irene was beside him most of the time, but she would leave the room for just a minute and he had no recollection of her ever having been there.

'I haven't seen you for years,' he'd screech at her.

Tom had always had such a friendly, easy-going personality, but the loss of so many things had left him much pricklier and less amiable than at any time before.

He could no longer drive, keep up with a normal conversation, recall the names of the people closest to him or do his precious drawing. He was still the person Irene loved, but he was not well. He was struggling, had lost his independence, his ability to cope and do things for himself, and all the treasured memories of their recent time together.

Four weeks later, when Tom was only 75 years and a month old, he had a heart-attack in the night. Irene heard a gasp for breath and a struggle next to her. She turned and put on the light to see him lying there, pale, not moving, but breathing gently. His eyes flickered as she jumped out of bed, and ran round to stand next to him.

'Shall I call an ambulance? Are you okay?'

His breathing seemed shallow, and soon he was gasping for breath.

'Don't leave me,' she said. 'Not after all we've been through, Tom. Please don't leave me now.'

His eyes closed as he gasped for breath, more shallowly this time. Irene issued a silent prayer to God, saying sorry for everything she'd done wrong, saying sorry for not completely loving this wonderful man like she should have. I promise, Lord, if you spare him, I'll devote my life to him, I'll do anything, anything. Please, please don't take him from me.

Tom opened his eyes and looked into the face of his wife. 'I adored you from the moment I first saw you,' he said. 'I'll love you forever. Please bury me in Gower. Please. Bury me in Gower.'

'I love you too, Tom. I love you more than anything in the world. You are the finest man I ever met.'

# CHAPTER 18

# $\mathcal{L}$landrindod Wells: Present Day

'Cheers,' I say, raising my glass and waiting for the others to raise theirs in reply.

'To the Mysterious Invitation Group,' says Simon.

'To us,' we all reply.

I look around the table...this rabble of individuals with so very little in common, flung together because of the fact that our relatives were once tangentially connected to a man who died.

'Thank you all so much for coming,' I say, taking on a leadership role. For some reason, it feels as if the whole thing has been pushed forward by me more than anyone else, so I feel the need to express gratitude to them for coming on the ride.

'The only person not here is Matt,' I say, suddenly realising that everyone else is here now.

'It's a real shame he couldn't come,' says Sally. Julie doesn't speak, but she says a great deal with her eyes, as she glares unremittingly at Mike and Polly, occasionally shaking her head as if to reconfirm to everyone that she's still in a state of shock and incomprehension about the situation.

Melissa and Bronwyn haven't joined us this evening. They've gone out into Llandrindod, to some lively bar, presumably to tell all their friends about this bizarre group of people they met. They seemed genuinely thrilled to have come with us on our little adventure to England, having never been out of the area before. Bronwyn even confessed that she'd never stayed in a hotel before, so the whole thing must have been an incredible adventure. I'm glad about that. I'm also glad we've managed to find some sort of solution to our problem. Even though it's not really a solution at all, and certainly not what we hope to achieve.

We're stuck with the fact that the family moved to America and settled there.

'Shall I call Matt?' I say. 'I could put him on loudspeaker so everyone can say hello to him?'

'Oh yes, do,' says Sally. 'Then he'll feel like he's here with us, and he'll know we haven't forgotten about him.'

We call his mobile, but get the answer phone, so we raise our glasses and offer a loud cheer to tell him we're thinking of him and wish he was with us.

I tell him I'll call him back when I'm at home and fully update him on what happened.

'I should ring the private detectives, shouldn't I?' I say. 'Just to tell them what we've managed to discover. I'll pass on the details of the Bellevue Hospital.'

'Yes, absolutely,' says Simon. 'I'm happy to call them if you want. They need to know about the research project conducted there decades ago, which saved the life of Tom's granddaughter.'

'I'll do it now,' I say. 'Before I forget.'

Again, I have the phone on loudspeaker, as I ring and ask the receptionist to put me through to Paul Dillon.

'I'm so sorry. I can't do that. Is there anyone else here who can help?'

'No, I really need to speak to him.'

I make faces at the others around the table, and Simon shrugs back at me, as if to say - what's wrong with them, why can't they just put you through to Paul, for goodness' sake?

'Can you tell me who's speaking?'

'My name's Mary Brown. It's quite a complicated story but he'll really want to hear what I've got to say. It's about Reginald Charters who died a year ago. I was invited to the funeral.'

'Oh, gosh - yes. I remember that.'

'So, can you put me through to him?'

'No, I'm afraid not. He passed a few days ago.'

'He passed?' I take the phone off the loudspeaker.

'Yes, he died. He had cancer. I don't know whether you knew that?'

'Oh, my goodness, I'm so sorry. I knew he was ill because I phoned a few days ago, and someone told me, but I didn't realise he was quite that bad. That's terrible news. I'm very sorry. Look, what I'll do is call back in a week or so.'

'Of course,' she says. 'Did you want details of the funeral? I know he was very fond of you, the way you stepped up to give a talk on the day of the funeral. That was an incredible gesture.'

'Thank you. Yes, let me have the funeral details…'

The lady on the phone tells me it will take place on Friday at 11am. 'It's at the same church as Reginald's funeral.'

'Thank you so much,' I say and tell her I'll see her on Friday.

Ted and Juan have their arms folded defensively. They've heard me make another plan, and they're clearly worried it's going to entail a drive across mountains and wild terrain in search of something that isn't there.

'Paul died,' I say bluntly, turning to the group. 'I'm really tempted to go to the funeral. It's at the same church as Reginald's.'

'What?' says Julie. 'What would possess you to go back to that godforsaken place?'

'I don't know, really. I just feel like it would be a nice thing to do. And there'll be people there from the area who we can talk to about what we discovered.'

'No,' says Ted. 'Honestly, love, let's just go home now.'

'I know it sounds mad, but it's not that far away.'

'It is quite far away,' says Mike. 'It's the other side of Wales.'

'Yeah, but it's not as far as we've been. We could go over there for the funeral, and then go on the train back from there. What do you think?'

Ted drops his head into his hands. I give him a little hug and tell him I'm glad he's so keen, which makes the others laugh. 'I know you probably think I'm mad but I'd so hoped to find the Gower family, and going back to where we all first met a year ago feels like a nice thing to do. Like some sort of resolution, even if it's not the one we were after.'

'If you want to go, we'll go,' says Ted.

'I want to go.'

'Actually, I'd quite like to go,' says Simon.

'Oh goodness, if you are going, I'll come,' says Sally.

'Well, I was going to get a lift back with you, Sally. So, I'll come too,' says Julie, in a move which surprises everyone.

We look at Mike. 'Yeah, why not,' he says. 'Let's go to Gower for the funeral.'

*Mysterious Invitation WhatsApp Group*

**Mary Brown:**

Hi Matt, I just left a message for you. Since then, we have decided to head to Gower. It's Paul Dillon's funeral on Friday (the private detective). It would be lovely if you could come. It's back at the church where Reginald's funeral was held. Call me when you can.

**Mike Sween:**

Come on, mate. Come and join us

**Simon Blake:**

It would be lovely to see you, if you can make it, Matt. Kind regards, Simon

**Sally Bramley:**

Hope to see you! X

# CHAPTER 19

# $\mathcal{G}$ower Farm Hotel: Present Day

It's very odd to be back at the Gower Farm Hotel, and it's strange to be going to the funeral of someone I know, but to which I haven't, strictly speaking, been invited.

Such a change from a year ago when we were invited to the funeral of someone we didn't know but to which we had been invited.

How about that for a story with a ridiculous beginning and a ridiculous end? We're soon going to be back in the same church, at the same place, with many of the same people.

'I feel a bit odd, now we're here at the hotel,' says Ted. 'Don't you?'

'No,' I say. 'I'm really glad we came.'

'But you didn't really know this guy. You only met him once.'

'Which is once more than I met the last guy whose funeral I came to here.'

'Well, I feel odd, even if you don't.'

The hotel looks a bit different from last time we were here, because lots of renovations are going on: there are workmen buzzing around the place, and the sound of hammers bashing and saws cutting as we get ready for the day ahead.

Ted looks very smart in his makeshift black outfit. I had to go to a shop in Llandrindod Wells and buy a black dress, because I obviously didn't think to bring a funeral outfit with me.

Shopping was an interesting experience. I don't think anyone in Llandrindod Wells is very fat because I struggled to find anything to fit me.

In the end I had to opt for a sort of tent creation. That was the only item that went anywhere near to getting over my tummy and my bum. It's made of linen and is deeply unflattering, so I am trying to make it look better with the addition of lots of makeup. But now I look like I'm going for a night out on the town, rather than going to a funeral, so I'm wiping some of the makeup off and trying to work out where the thin line is between demure respectability and high-end hooker. Funnily enough, the line is not as clear as you might imagine it would be.

There's a knock on the door, and I answer to see Sally standing there, dressed in her black and looking really lovely. 'Oh, you look nice,' she says.

'No, you look nice,' I reply. 'I look odd. This was the only thing I could find to wear. And now I think I might have too much makeup on.'

'Stop it. You look perfect. Absolutely perfect. Oh, and your husband looks handsome.'

'Why thank you, ma'am,' says Ted, leading us down the rickety stairs that I first walked down a year ago, in a state of utter confusion, and some trepidation, out to the side of the building toward the church.

We walk in and join the other Mysterious Invitation people, so we're all sitting together on one pew. I spot Matt at the end, and wave and blow kisses until Ted tells me to stop.

'Inappropriate,' he whispers, as I drop my hand.

The service is quite long, and some of the readings are in Welsh, which doesn't allow us to feel part of the whole thing. But it's lovely and warm, and there are loads of people there, including the tallest vicar I've ever seen. He must be about seven foot tall. There's clearly there's a lot of affection for the local private detective who has been working on the High Street for his entire life. I spend time trying to work out who the people in the church are, but it's very hard when everyone's sitting there in black, crying.

So, I decide to relax and enjoy it as much as I can. After the service there's a burial, but it's for close family and friends, so instead we're invited back to Paul's house, where there's a small buffet and the chance to share memories about him. We all stand together, we interlopers who've travelled across Wales to be here. Then we walk as one behind the crowds of people leaving the church and on to Paul's house.

'Hello, don't think we've met,' says a voice, as a man in a green suit catches up with us. 'I'm John, Paul's brother.'

'Oh, it's lovely to meet you. I'm so sorry for your loss.'

'Thank-you, dear, but I refuse to be downbeat about it. He lived a good, long life and had been very ill for a long time. In the end, his passing was a mercy, he was in so much pain. Now's the time to celebrate a life well-lived. That's why I refuse to wear black.'

I introduce myself and the others to him, and begin to tell the story of how we all met Paul.

'Oh, my goodness. I heard about that. Paul told me all about it. What an astonishing thing to happen. Did they ever find the other family? The one that was missing on the funeral day?'

'No, they didn't. They were called the Gower family, and we've been rushing around this past week, to see whether we can find them.'

'Any luck?'

'No, we started in Llandrindod Wells which was the last address we had for them, and found they'd gone to Southsea, then to Brighton, then to America. We went to Southsea and Brighton, but drew the line at making a trans-Atlantic search for them.'

John smiles. 'You've been on quite an adventure. There might be someone here who knows what happened to them. It would be worth having a chat with a few people.'

'I will,' I say. 'But I might have a bite to eat first.'

We all move through to the buffet, and join the queue for food, then find a quiet corner in which to eat.

'Shall we head off after this?' says Ted. 'It's a long train ride home, and it would be nice to be back before it's too late.'

'Sure,' I say. 'But give me ten minutes. I'll go and circulate and find out whether there's anyone here who knows the Gower family, then we'll go. Okay?'

'Sure,' he says.

I put my plate down and walk back into the main room, scanning the people who are standing around, before moving up to one small group and introducing myself.

'I wonder - you don't know the Gower family, by any chance, do you? They used to live here, on the farm, many years ago.'

'Sorry, no,' says the woman, and the others in her group shake their heads.

'They owned Gower Farm?'

'I'm sorry, I don't know them.'

I slip away and edge my way into a group of older people who might have known Tom and Irene, or known of them.


'Oh, yes. My parents knew them when they were here. They moved to north Wales, I think.'

'Yes,' I say. 'Then they moved to England.'

'To England?'

'Yes, down to the south coast. Then they moved to New York.'

'No...' comes the reply. 'Goodness me, weren't they adventurous.'

'Their granddaughter wasn't well, so they moved there to get treatment for her.'

'Yes, that's right,' comes a strong, deep voice from beside me. It's the vicar, smiling down at me from his considerable height. 'They moved back to Wales after that.'

'Really? Did they? Really?'

'Yes, Tom Gower was buried here. It must have been 25 or 30 years ago now. His wife settled somewhere near Port Eynon,

I think. That's a little place on the coast. Irene lived a long life and only died a few years ago.'

'Gosh. Are other members of the family around?'

'TJ is still alive, but in a nursing home, I think. I know that Yvonne, his wife, died years ago. His son Andrew is living in Germany, but Andrew's sons, Eddie and Charlie, are in the country. They have just finished university.'

'Gosh. So, when Paul was hunting for the family last year, they were right under his nose?'

'Well, no, the boys weren't around here then - they were away at uni. Paul wouldn't have known that they had come back to the area. They were buried here because they both wanted to be near the farm, but their funerals were in Port Eynon. No one realised the family was back in Wales. I didn't until I saw the graves and met Charlie and Eddie there.'

'Gosh. One of the reasons I am keen to find them is to make sure they know about the money that has been left to them. Is anyone in touch with Andrew or his kids? Is there any way you could pass a note to them if I left one with you?'

'Or you could go and talk to them. Charlie and Eddie are staying at the Gower House Hotel while they are back from uni. They're helping with refurbishments there.'

# CHAPTER 20

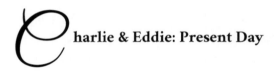
harlie & Eddie: Present Day

I head back to Ted, and the group, and tell them the news.

'I promise we'll go after this, Ted, but I have to go and meet Tom and Irene's great grandchildren first, after everything we've been through to try and find them.'

'Sure,' he says.

We all gather our coats and bags, walk back to the hotel, and I approach the receptionist and ask her where I might find the Gower brothers, then we all take a seat in reception to await their arrival.

It's not long before two tall, handsome and charming young men appear in reception, eager to talk to us about their family.

I explain to them all about the funeral a year ago. I tell them the story about Marco going to work on their great-grandfather's farm and how kind Tom and Irene were to him. I tell them about Marco's theatrical son, Joe, who was shunned by society so changed his name to Reginald and decided to hand his wealth over to those who had treated him and his father well.

They take the news of the money being left to them with wide-eyed amazement.

'Are you sure? I mean - I never even met this guy Reginald, or his dad.'

'Nor us,' I say.

'We went to the funeral and no one there had met Reginald,' explains Simon. 'It was the most peculiar experience.'

'God, I can imagine,' say Charlie and Eddie.

'Do you want to come with us, to the graveyard? We were about to go down there and put flowers on our grandma Yvonne's grave. Our great-grandma and grandpa are right next to her.'

'Gosh, yes, I'd love to,' I say, and we all walk over to the graveyard next to the churchyard.

We follow Charlie and Eddie as they walk past the gravestones and under a little archway through to a second graveyard, and follow them to the graves of Tom and Irene.

'Here,' says Charlie, and I actually gasp when I see two headstones, standing right next to one another. At the bottom of each one it says: Unedig gyda'n gilydd yn y nefoedd.

'What does that mean?' I ask Charlie.

'United again in heaven,' he says, and I start to cry a little.

I know it sounds silly because I didn't know Tom and Irene at all. In fact, I'd never even been to Wales before we received the invitation to the funeral a year ago, but I just feel so glad that it worked out for those two in the end, despite some hair-raising moments along the way.

'It looks like Irene realised how much she loved Tom in the final years of their lives. That's really touching,' I say, while the others look at me as if I've entirely lost my mind. I seem to be so much more invested in this family than anyone else is. I love that they are now together for eternity...let's just hope that Mark isn't wherever they're going, or it all might go pear-shaped again.

Charlie and Eddie lay flowers on the graves, and we stand back and watch in silence. I cast an eye along the group...the Mysterious Invitation gang all together at Tom and Irene's graves a year after the funeral. There's something quite magical about it all.

Then we all walk back through the archway, past the church, and back up the road toward the hotel.

'What do you think you'll do with the money?' I ask.

'We won't get it, will we?' says Charlie. 'I thought the money was for Tom and Irene.'

'No, it's very much for you. Reginald made a point of stating that the money should go to the youngest living relatives. That's you two. He'd be very keen for you to have it. You'll be able to set yourselves up for life.'

They look at me, then at each other, and then back at me again.

'Really, the money is for us? Literally for us, and not a sort of pot of money for the family to share?'

'Nope. All for you. You've got your great grandparents to thank. They were both so kind to Reginald's father, that Reginald felt moved to leave a lot of money to you.'

'It's lovely to hear something like that about one of your relatives,' says Charlie.

'I know,' I say. 'When we were at the funeral a year ago, we all said the same. I'm very proud that someone I'm related to behaved so kindly that a dying man's last wish was to reward him.'

Once we are back at the hotel, I feel like it's not our place to stay any longer, so we decide to head off, and go into town to Joe's ice cream parlour and experience one of his gorgeous ice creams before getting the train home.

We bid farewell to Charlie and Eddie, and all exchange numbers, then we head off to indulge ourselves...all six of us, and our entourage, off to enjoy the creamy Italian taste that we have heard so much about.

We seat ourselves in the fifties-style ice cream parlour and order the biggest ice creams they have.

I can't tell you how beautiful it tastes: rich and creamy and just gorgeous, full of fresh strawberries, nuts and sauce. Ted has the fudge one, and it's not only full of fudge, it's also packed with fudge brownie, toffee sauce, pecan nuts and tonnes of caramel and chocolate.

'Best ice cream ever,' says Ted. 'Really first class.'

Then we all raise our ice cream dishes in a toast.

'To Reginald.'

'I know this has been a really unusual trip,' I say to Ted, whilst the others chat amongst themselves. 'And you and Juan must have been bored out of your mind at times, but I'm really glad it ended like this.'

'What? In an ice-cream shop?'

'Well - yes - I'm very glad about that, but I'm mainly pleased that our journey finished with us finding those lovely young men. I feel like our cross-country trip was all worth it.'

'Yeah,' says Ted, licking out his bowl like a four-year-old. 'I had my doubts when we drove to Brighton in that pink hair-dressing van, but it all turned out well in the end. Well done, Mary Brown. I salute you.'

# EPILOGUE

$\mathcal{A}$ couple of months after our trip to Wales, I am woken early on a Saturday morning by a text.

*Hello. Do you remember us? It's Charlie and Eddie Gower here. I hope you're well and made it back home to England safely. We just wanted to share some news with you.*

*We've decided to put our money together and we're going to buy Gower Farm.*

*It means we'll own the farm that our great grandpa had when he was younger...the one that Marco came over to in the war. We thought Reginald would approve.*

*We're also going to send money over to our auntie at the hospital in New York.*

*You and Ted are welcome to come to our farm, anytime. Tell Ted to bring his wellies though, because we'll be putting him to work!*

*Thanks for making all that effort to find us.*

*Please come and visit us!*
*Lots of love,*

*Charlie and Eddie Gower*

Bernice Bloom

## Fancy reading the next book?

This is the next book in the series...featuring a trip to Charlie and Eddie's farm:

My Book

Made in the USA
Columbia, SC
28 April 2021